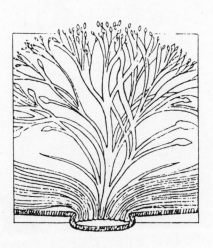

# THE
# PRINCESS HOPPY

OTHER BOOKS BY JACQUES ROUBAUD
IN ENGLISH TRANSLATION

*Our Beautiful Heroine*
*Hortense Is Abducted*
*Some Thing Black*
*The Great Fire of London*
*Hortense in Exile*

Jacques Roubaud

# THE
# PRINCESS HOPPY

## OR
## THE TALE OF LABRADOR

Translated by Bernard Hœpffner

Dalkey Archive Press

Originally published by Hatier. © 1990 by Hatier.
English translation © 1993 by Bernard Hœpffner.
All rights reserved.

Chapters 4, 6, and 8 first appeared in English translation (in slightly
different form) in *Conjunctions* 18 (1992).

Publication of this book was made possible in part by grants from the
French Ministry of Culture, the National Endowment for the Arts, the
Illinois Arts Council, and the Florence J. Gould Foundation.

Dalkey Archive Press
Fairchild Hall
Illinois State University
Normal, IL 61790

*Printed on permanent/durable acid-free paper and bound in the
United States of America.*

# Contents

# THE
# PRINCESS HOPPY

# Chapter 0

# Some Indications about What the Tale Says

**The one telling the tale**

1    It is the tale that tells, and the one telling the tale is the tail, the Tail of Labrador. Thus the tale is said to be the Tale of Labrador.

2    When the tale says what the tale says, the tale tells you: here is what the tale says. Who is then speaking, the tale? Yes, but don't ever forget that the tale is the tale of Labrador.

3    This is certainly not the first tale told by a tail. But most probably it is the first tale of Labrador told by a tail of Labrador.

4    You might find it difficult to believe that the $\frac{\text{tale}}{\text{tail}}$ is the author of the story; and if you believe this, maybe you are wrong to do so.

5    *Careful!* Do not trust tales that tell you their tale as if the tale were the author of the tale. Distrust even more the Tail of Labrador.

**That the tale is true**

6    The tale always tells the truth. What the tale says is true because the tale tells it. Some say that the tale tells the truth because what the tale tells is true. Others that the tale doesn't tell

the truth because truth is not a tale. But in reality what the tale tells is true of what the tale tells that what the tale tells is true. This is why the tale tells the truth.

7   The tale tells the truth. This does not mean that the Tail of Labrador tells the truth. The truth of the tale is not always the truth of the tail. The tale is nevertheless true.

8   What the tale tells happened while the tale was telling it. It even happened while the tale was telling what the tale was telling. This is why it is so true.

9   Often the tale lies            the tale lies often
     the tale often lies           often.

10   There are two tales in the tale: the tale told by the tale and the telling of what the tale tells. It adds up in fact to much more than two tales.

11   The truth of the tale is in the tale. Which tale? Well, in the tale and in the tale recounted by the tale. Thus is the truth of the tale the truth of the truth.

12   When the tale lies, and it will eventually lie as it tells the truth, the tale will be finished.

**What there is in the tale**

13   In this tale there is what there is in a tale, whatever makes a tale a tale. It can be defined as being what there is in a tale, and as this tale is a tale, all of this can be found in this tale. This is what there is in this tale.

14   There is in this tale a princess and her dog. The name of the princess is Hoppy. Thus the title of the tale is: *The Princess*

*Hoppy.* The name of the dog is kept privy for security reasons.

15  There are in this tale kings queens and one astronomer. There are lots of other people as well. Everybody's name is in the index. The names of the kings, the names of the queens are in a separate index.

16  There is in this tale information about the weather. There are passages and passages about journeys. They extend to pages and pages. They can be omitted at the first reading. There is a bit of everything in the tale.

17  *What there isn't:* in this tale there are no, I repeat, in this tale there are no suspenders. That's what there are none of in the tale.

**When one tells the tale. When one tells you the tale**

18  When one tells the tale it must be told in such a way that it appears to be the tale which tells the tale. And this is normal after all as it is the tale which tells the tale.

19  *Careful!* Careful! the tale sometimes requires close attention.

20  At times the tale gives false indications. In that case the tale says that the tale gives false indications. At times.

21  *Language:* The tale is said to be in the language of the tale. The language of the tale is English. The language of the tale is **Dog** as well. What is English? the language of the tale. What is **Dog**?

22  *Anticipations.* But let's not anticipate.

23  *To tell the tale:* ask for a glass of wine. If there is no wine, or if you don't drink wine, don't tell the tale. Unless you still want to tell the tale.

24  While telling the tale, tell, tell the tale. Do not tell "About Materialism" by Philippe Sollers or "Prayer to Go to Heaven Together with the Donkeys." Tell the tale.

## To whom the tale tells

25  The tale is being told to you. Who then are you? Those to whom the tale tells. If the tale is being told to you, it means you.

26  The tale tells for those who are more or less than twenty, more or less than sixty, who are seventeen or more, thirty-one or less, forty-one or more, fourteen or less. It is always the same tale. But not always the same people.

27  This tale is for grasshoppers. This tale is for one particular grasshopper particularly.

28  Those to whom the tale tells, if they are listening to the tale, let them be thanked. The thanks are in the tale. To hear them, one must listen.

29  In those days the tale was everywhere and all had access to it. Which days?

30  Now those for whom the tale is the tale are in the tale. For whom is the tale?

31  *The last indication:*

t' cea uc tscl rs
n neo rt aluot
ia ouna s ilel-
-rc oal ei ntoi.

(it's in **Dog**).

# Chapter 1

## Plots and Pots

1    In those days the Princess had a dog and four uncles who were kings. The first king was named **Aligoté**. He was king of **Zambezi** and surrounding regions. The second king was named **Babylas**. He was king of **Ypermétrope** and surrounding regions. The third king was named **Eleonor** (without an e) and the fourth **Imogène**.

Eleonor (without an e) and Imogène were not just any old kings. They each had a very large and beautiful kingdom but the tale does not at present say where for security reasons.

2    The tale says what it should when it should and the tale now says that Aligoté occasionally paid a visit to Babylas in his kingdom or to Eleonor in his or else to Imogène and the tale says that likewise it happened that Babylas would pay a visit to Eleonor in his kingdom or to Imogène in his or else to Aligoté and moreover the tale says that Eleonor sometimes visited Imogène in his kingdom Aligoté in his or else Babylas that at times Imogène went to visit Aligoté in his kingdom Babylas in his or else Eleonor. At any rate this is what the tale says.

3    And when King Aligoté was at Babylas with the Princess and her dog and the Princess had gone down to the lawn just below the front steps to play ball with her dog King Babylas would say to Aligoté, "My dear cousin, let us go into my study." But here the tale ceases to talk about Aligoté and Babylas and goes back to Eleonor who has gone to visit Imogène in his kingdom.

4   And the tale says that when King Eleonor had gone to see Imogène with the Princess and her dog and when the Princess had gone down to the lawn below the front steps to play ball with her dog, King Imogène would say to Eleonor, "My dear cousin, let us go into my study." And when both Eleonor and Imogène were in the study and they had turned the key they started plotting.

5   It has to be said that in those days the Princess had a lot of worries. For every time one of the four kings her uncles (Aligoté for example) paid a visit to another of her four uncles, a king (Imogène for example) in his kingdom, and they entered the study after having sent her to play ball with her dog on the lawn below the front steps and they turned the key, they started plotting. They plotted against one of the four kings who were her four uncles. And what's more, it wasn't rare for one of the kings (Eleonor for example) to pay a visit to himself in his kingdom, escorted by the Princess and the dog and, after having sent the Princess to play ball, to shut himself in his study to plot. It added up to quite a few plots and the dog was fed up with playing ball.

6   The tale reminds you here that when King Uther Pendragon fell sick of the malady of death he called for the Princess and her dog as well as for his four nephews Imogène, Aligoté, Babylas, Eleonor (without an e) and he told them: "My children, my child, my dog, I know I am going to die. I have been struck by death and there is no cure. When I am dead," he added, turning toward the four kings, his nephews, "I know very well what will happen: Imogène, for example, will pay a visit to Babylas in his kingdom, with the Princess and her dog, and what will they do? I am going to tell you. They will send the Princess to play ball with her dog on the lawn below the front steps, they will enter the study, turn the key, and start plotting. Against whom? I don't know, I don't give a damn and it's all the same to me. Okay I cannot stop you from doing so. I have been struck by death, I'm

going to kick the bucket, Merlin has told me, nothing can be done about it. But there exists a sacred rule established since time immemorial by Saint Benedict and which you will swear to respect for your plotting. Okay?" and Uther Pendragon continued in a loud voice:

7  *Rule of Saint Benedict: Let there be three kings among you four: the first king, the second king, the third king. The first king is any king, the second king is any king* . . . "Can the second king be the same as the first?" interrupted Eleonor. "Of course," said Uther . . . *the third king is any king. So:*

*The king against whom the first king plots when he pays a visit to the king against whom the second king plots when he pays a visit to the third must be precisely the same king who is plotted against by the king against whom the first king plots when he pays a visit to the second, when he pays a visit to the third.* Okay?" said Uther, "but that is not all":

*When a king pays a visit to another king they will always plot against the same king. And if two distinct kings pay a visit to the same third, the first will never plot against the same king as the second. Finally every king will be plotted against at least once a year in the study of each of the kings.* "I have spoken," said Uther. "Okay?" said Uther. And he died.

8  The tale now says that the Princess and her dog would have liked very much to know against whom her uncle Imogène plotted when he paid a visit to her uncle Babylas and they shut themselves up in the study. And, in a more general way, the Princess would have liked very much to know, for example, if, given any two of her uncles, the one against whom the first plotted when he paid a visit to the second would be the same, or not, as the one against whom the second plotted when he paid a visit to the first. "Yes," said the dog. He had picked up the ball on the lawn below the front steps and was holding it, drooling, in his mouth. "Don't speak with your mouth full," said the Princess, and she added,

"and why so, if you please?" **"Because,"** said the dog, **"a rou ith our eleents is autoatiall outatie."** He generally excelled in **Dog**-English translation when he had a ball across his canines. "Ah," said the Princess. It was time for tea. And they walked up to the kitchen where Queen Ingrid was expecting them.

9  Now, says the tale, Kings Aligoté, Imogène, Babylas and Eleonor were first cousins and they had married four first cousins. These were Queens Adirondac, Botswanna, Eleonore (with an e) and Ingrid. Queen Adirondac was born Zibeline y Zanivcovette. Queen Botswanna was born Yolanda and Ygrometria. Queens Eleonore (with an e) and Ingrid were born as well but the tale does not say where for security reasons. The tale goes straight to the point and says that when Aligoté for example paid a visit to Imogène for the sole purpose of plotting with him according to the rule of Saint Benedict, Queen Adirondac paid a visit to Queen Ingrid in her kitchen. And while the kings *plotted*, the queens *potted* jam. To such good purpose that when he left, King Aligoté could put a parcel in the mail containing whatever pots had not been eaten during the tea prepared for the queen who was the wife of the king against whom they had the same afternoon in Imogène's study plotted. And that is how things went.

10 Everything in the kingdoms went on in the best possible way. The kings plotted, the queens potted, the Princess played ball with her dog on the perfectly green lawn below the front steps, the dog translated from **Dog** to English and from English to **Dog**, when one morning...

# Chapter 2

## Bilberries and Beryl

To the best
the most cruel
of Princesses
these bilberries of my suffering.
The Tail of Labrador

### 1   One morning

It was a beautiful morning in May and the birds were singing deliciously in four trees. Some sang in Celtic (Irish, Scottish Gaelic, Gaelic, Cornish or Breton), the others in Romance languages (*oïl*, *oc*, *si*, Catalan, Spanish or Gallego-Portuguese). None sang in **Dog**. In a pine tree an English squirrel was reading the *Times*. From time to time he took two hazelnuts from his library, while browsing through the society column on the first page. He nibbled one of them and threw the other one in the river from which a salmon jumped to catch it before it had touched the water. It was a moment of sweetness beyond words.

### 2   Beryl

But Princess Hoppy wasn't happy. She had this same morning come with her uncle Imogène on a visit and instead of quietly playing ball on the lawn with her dog who was looking forward to a game, she had to look after her cousin. Now her cousin, whose name was Beryl, was a doe, a white doe, white everywhere but for one or two small places that were pink. She wore black patent dancing shoes with large violet eyes. And she refused to play ball with the Princess and her dog, saying with her acid-drop voice while opening her large wet eyes: "Do excuse me, but I must stay immaculately white." And for the same reason she wouldn't go swimming in the river. Nor would she play G W D D B W L L between the four trees (the pine, the hazelnut, the cypress and the coconut tree) where the birds went on singing imperturbably. The Princess didn't know what to do.

## 3   The bone collection

The dog wasn't happy either as he had buried some bones under the trees and he was afraid that they would be stolen. He permanently kept 4 x 4 bones under the trees of each of the four identical lawns of the Princess's uncles. Every time he came on a visit to one of the Princess's uncles, he dug up the most ancient bone in his collection to gnaw it, and replaced it with a new bone. But he knew himself to be, alas, surrounded by enemies only waiting for the propitious moment to make away with his most precious item that is to say precisely the oldest bone in his collection. So he buried the four bones protected by the roots of each tree at various depths and always following a different order of the four bones he was especially fond of at that time: a bone from a leg of antelope — the bone of a bear — an elephant bone — and the bone of an iguanodon. "Antelope for taste," he would say, "bear to make the hair impervious to rain, and the elephant to acquire an infinite wisdom and sagacity." (What about the iguanodon, will you ask? Ha-ha, I was sure you would ask that question.) Moreover, as soon as he had dug up the oldest bone of his collection and a new bone had become, ipso facto, the oldest bone in his collection, he shifted them round with the same movement under their trees, the better to mix the trails: **"I kow vey well i's useess,"** he'd say to the Princess while shrugging his shoulders, **"ut I ill hae one hat i ould."**

*13*

# 4 Gifts and lawns

The tale says at this point that when Kings Babylas, Eleonor (without an e), Imogène and Aligoté got married, King Uther Pendragon wanted to give them a present. As each of them was his favorite nephew, he decided to give them each the same present and after having thought a long time again decided to offer them each a lawn. "Qu'en penses-tu, chère, est-ce une bonne idée?" ["what do you think, dear, is it a good idea?"], he said to Ygerne, his wife. "Certainement Uther" ["if you think so, Uther, it must be so"], answered Ygerne, who never got used to adding Pendragon to Uther after he had decided to append to his name that of his beloved and deceased twin brother (in that order). Uther called for his landscape gardener and told him: "Sire Architect, I want each lawn to be exactly 35 meters long and 43 meters wide." "But, Sire," objected the architect, "a lawn, even rectangular, cannot be wider than it is long." "Never mind," said Uther, "it will remind them of a billiard cloth. And don't forget," he added, "to give them each a perimeter of 157 meters. Oh, I know," he went on when he saw that the architect was again ready to protest, "I know very well that 35 + 43 + 35 + 43 make 156. But it will give them a meter to spare for the hem." And so it was done. The castles rose at the edges of the lawns. They were 35 meters long. The rivers ran parallel to the pediments of the castles on the other side of the grass and the trees were planted in the widths: the albino pine faced the Iceland cypress and the barometer-hazelnut the eglantine-coconut. Uther Pendragon had insisted on having the coconuts trees crossed with eglantine so that the coconuts would grow thorns to protect them from the craniums on which they would fall during the rainy season.

# 5 The Princess ponders

The Princess was pondering. The almond berries, she said to

herself, are ripe on the banks of the river. Across the river, between the river and the path, the embraves are equally ripe. On the other side of the path, there is the forest and in the forest the bilberries are ripe. To cross the river, there is Uncle Babylas's duck-boat. To cross the path, there is the four-color traffic lights and the crosswalk. Why shouldn't we go and pick almond berries, embraves and bilberries for Aunt Ingrid's compote?

## 6    Yes, but

Yes, but, the Princess said to herself, Uncle Babylas's duck-boat cannot at the same time carry the dog, the almond berries and Beryl. If I take the three of them with me, it sinks. If I take two, it pitches, which isn't much better. If I leave my dog on the bank with Beryl while I carry the almond berries to the other side, he will rush at her and lick her all over: I can't persuade him that she is not covered with ice cream and he wants to know whether it's vanilla ice cream or lemon sorbet. Yes, but, let's suppose that I leave Beryl with the almond berries while I cross over with the dog, she will stuff herself with berries and will get stains all over. Furthermore, to cross the path, I will have to hold their hand (or paw) and as one of my hands will be busy with the basket of almond berries if not with the one of embraves, how will I manage it?

While she was thus pondering, the dog busied himself with his weekly bone-moves. The almond berries went on ripening. Beryl was sitting on a cushion of puce velvet that had been sewn by her mother, Queen Botswanna. She waited with great patience, all the while carefully checking the various elements of whiteness of which she was made up so that not one leaf, drop of water, or blade of grass would come to offend the perfection. The window of Uncle Babylas's study was partly open and fragments of the conversation could be heard: "But I cannot really," said Imogène, ". . . and on Sunday, no less! You can't be serious! I categorically ref . . ."

That's not all, the Princess went on in her interior monologue; with all that, how will I bring the bilberries back? She made a dispirited gesture. But she immediately pulled herself together: "Fiddlesticks!" she said to herself, "it doesn't matter! My dog is bound to come up with a solution!"

## 7  Boats

Uncle Babylas's boat, the same in any case as the respective boats of Eleonor (without an e), Imogène and Aligoté, was pulled by four ducks. Each duck had been provided with a small electric chafing dish containing anthracite ovoids. When starting the boat, the ducks pressed on a nickel-plated switch placed at the back of the heater, thus rapidly bringing the anthracite to incandescence. Then, grabbing their heaters between their experienced palms, they opened them slightly with a small screw situated, this time, in front. Upon contact of the water with the burning anthracite, a hissing could be heard and a powerful jet of steam rose around the small craft. That steam, let us add quickly, was of no use as far as locomotion was concerned, this being much more simply provided by purple cysemus straps passing over their shoulders; but Babylas (as well as Imogène, Aligoté and Eleonor) could thus without lying answer the question: And what about you, what type of boat do you have? with a "Oh, just a steamboat," an answer he found much more stylish than "Oh, just a duck-boat."

When not in use, the boat was generally docked in the water lily marina to which the ducks would gain access by each dropping a penny in the cup of one of the water lily leaves that barred the entrance. As four hours were necessary for the leaves to regain their initial position, this simple and ingenious device gave Babylas the use of a docking area that was not only private (there was only space for one boat, his) but a profitable business as well. Of course the pennies dropped to the bottom, but each year he would have the bottom dragged (during the water lilies' vacation) to retrieve his money, except for a few coins deducted by the salmon for his own expenses. When she stepped into the boat, Beryl carefully lifted the seat cover at the back to check that not one speck of dust, not one stain of duck oil, would damage her great white silence. After having sat down, she glanced pensively at the uneven surface of the water barely perturbed from time to time by the salmon's curiosity. "I hope you are not forgetting," she said to the Princess, "that I must stay immaculately white."

## 8   Balance

The dog went to sit at the Princess's foot with a sigh of relief. He was fairly proud of his morning: thanks to him the four baskets (almond berries, embraves, banana-bilberries and indigo-bilberries) had been filled with berries and nicely lined up along the path while waiting for the time to return. He had picked 899 almond berries, the Princess 101 and Beryl 3 (for reason of whiteness). He had then picked 899 embraves, the Princess 101 and Beryl 3. The embraves had been carried across the path following a method known to him only. The almond berries as well had crossed the road after the river. The dog had then picked 899 banana-bilberries, and the same of indigo-bilberries, the Princess 101 of each and Beryl 3. A little sun filtered through the trees. He stretched on his back in the moss and pulled down his ears over his eyes to protect himself from the light ("Close your shutters," the Princess would say). He vaguely hoped that before giving the signal for going back, the Princess would lean down and place a sloppy kiss on the warm fur of his cheeks.

## 9   Traffic lights

It was 11:44 exactly when the Princess arrived in front of the crossing served by Uncle Babylas's four-color traffic lights which protected pedestrians wanting to cross over. In one hand she held the basket of (banana-) bilberries and with the other Beryl, whose large violet eyes were open to her still immaculate whiteness. The dog waited, looking after the three other fruit baskets. The tale is very specific about the time being 11:44, and if the tale specifies the time, it is because the time must be specified by the tale as it holds some importance in the tale in the same way as everything it deals with and which it reports as it should, not being used to waste neither its time nor that of its listeners in idle digressions and superfluous embellishments. So if the tale now says it was 11:44, it means it was 11:44. At any rate it was now 11:45. The red light became propitious. It has to be said that the traffic on the path which separated the forest from the river and went along parallel to them in Uncle Babylas's plain wasn't excessive. The **Alcalde's** coach went by at eight o'clock; that of the **baker** at nine; at eleven o'clock came the mounted **emissary**; then an **Ilongot** at eleven, but on foot. At times a **road man** was seen in the afternoon pushing the hundredweight of his barrow full of loose chippings from one hectometric milestone to another. At times, even less frequently, a **traveler** equipped with a useless Michelin road map. The risk of collision was indeed minimal; it might have stayed that way for a long time if, during the first February of the year of the tale, young **Bartleby,** hedgehog, residing in *Uncle Babylas's Forest*, hadn't announced in the *Times* his engagement with young **Briolanja**, hedgehog, domiciled at the *place called The Embraves*, between the path and the river in front of the castle.

Now, Bartleby was seriously nearsighted, as are all hedgehogs; and to top it all, extraordinarily absentminded. He thus ran terrible risks when crossing the path without precautions to visit his fiancée. The tale takes advantage of the opportunity here given it to protest once more (see the first three parts of the tale) with the utmost vigor against the hedgehogicide of which drivers are guilty on French roads, with the collusion of the authorities. It is a disgrace to our country.

Warned of the danger by the Princess and the dog, King

Babylas had immediately put up the traffic lights the tale is presently talking about. This had four colors: vermilion, yellow, apple green, gray and a delicate flesh tint (this doesn't add up to five colors: gray isn't a color). Bartleby was indeed only responsive to the last of these tints which, he said, reminded him of the tiny tongue of his fiancée Briolanja.

Bartleby thus crossed when the light was pink, the Princess when it was vermilion; vehicles, horses and pedestrians crossed when it was apple green; no one crossed when it was yellow; **snails, ants** and **grasshoppers** when the light was gray. A sign in 1003 languages had been installed for foreigners and gave the instructions to be followed. And when King Babylas walked on his path for his postprandial stroll, the four colors shone at the same time. "I am the owner of a set of four-color traffic lights!" he liked to repeat when, escorted by his Alcalde, he attended international congresses for the twinning of castles. It was 11:45. The traffic light turned vermilion.

## 10   Event

It was 11:45 and the traffic light turned vermilion. The Princess, holding Beryl with one hand and the basket of (banana-) bilberries with the other, stepped onto the crosswalk to cross the path.

At that moment a thundering noise was heard and a horseman appeared in the distance. He was clad in black armor. His horse was black. The spear he held in his right hand was black. His left hand was covered with a black glove. His horse galloped at tremendous speed, raising a cloud of **white** dust that rose up to the **blue** sky then fell back slowly onto the **green** grass. In an instant, amazingly brief, he crossed the distance separating him from Uncle Babylas's traffic lights but, instead of stopping, which he should have done after reading the sign in 1003 languages especially and visibly placed there for his attention and which indicated that the color vermilion was reserved for the Princess, instead, I say, of making a dead stop in front of the

*19*

crosswalk, he went over it without diminishing his speed by an iota, and at the exact moment he was going over it, leaning on the left side of his black saddle, he seized poor Beryl round the waist and, tearing her from the Princess's hand, threw her gasping across his horse which continued its insane way on Uncle Babylas's path, soon hidden inside the cloud of **white** dust that rose as he sped along up to the **blue** sky, then fell back indifferent onto the **green** grass of the plain. It was 11:46.

The sound of the black hooves died away in the distance. The traffic light turned a "delicate flesh tint." But they were leaving behind, these hooves, a scene of desolation: the bilberries had been spilled onto the crosswalk; the Princess was dumbfounded with surprise; the dog was barking courageously.

At that moment, suddenly surging in turn from out of the cloud of dust which hadn't had enough time to settle but walking **the other way**, appeared a young man. He grasped at a glance the sorry scene before him and, understanding immediately that an event had just taken place, he cried out "What is it? what's the matter? what has happened?" "Who are you?" said the Princess. "I am an **Astronomer** and I come from **Baghdad**."

# Chapter 3

# The Astronomer's Adventure

## 1    Gardens

"My parents were poor but honest." "Skip all that," the Princess said hastily. "When I was seventeen," continued the young man, "I passed the BIAE with flying colors." "I beg your pardon?" said the dog courteously and in English. "Yes, the BIAE, the Baghdad Ilozoïst Astronomers Examination. There I spent the two most marvelous years of my life. Both the observatory and our school, which abutted on it, were situated inside the hanging gardens of Baghdad." "Excuse me," said the Princess, "I believed the hanging gardens to be in Babylon." "You're very much mistaken there!" exclaimed the young man. "You are, alas, the victim of a fallacious though prevalent impression generated by the deceitful and shameless touristic propaganda of the Babylonians, who, between you and me, are second-rate astronomers, and not much better as gardeners. Believe me, the only hanging gardens worthy of the name are those of my native city. But judge for yourself as you listen to my description:

## 2    Strawberry plants and tulips

"When at dawn I would finally leave my telescope after a night studiously spent examining the Canis constellation, for example, I always took a few steps along the paths surrounding the garden where, from the top of the asbestos parapets—" "I am very sorry to interrupt you again," said the dog, still very courteously and in English, "but why asbestos?" "To stop the after-

21

noon sun from setting fire to the emeralds embedded there." "I see," said the dog (when he didn't see at all). "Whence, as I was saying," went on the young man, "one descries the old town still coiled in the arms of the Indus." "Oh!" exclaimed the dog, but he didn't continue. "A fresh perfume emanated from the (numerous) clumps of asphodel. At my feet stretched a soft carpet of strawberry plants like babouches and I only had to bend down to borrow one of their succulent fruits, still iced with morning frost. Not far away could be heard something like a polyphony of young voices: 'Six times one, six; six times two, twelve; six times three, zero; six times four. . . .' " "Six times four, six," interjected the dog mechanically. "It was a bed of small arithmetician tulips reciting their multiplication table modulo eighteen. But what's the point of describing to you all the marvels enclosed in these gardens which I will in any case, alas, never again see?" And he discreetly wiped away a tear. "Two years went by, swifter than a lunar eclipse or a precession of the equinoxes, and then, after having brilliantly passed my BATD, I was appointed trainee ADAICCITOB (i.e., Attendant Dusting Assistant In Charge of Calculation of Imaginary Trajectories to the Observatory of Baghdad), and was asked to keep an eye on the Andromeda nebula which, apparently, nurtured some escape plans. I was happy with my work, and my senior in rank, the ADAICCQTOB fourth grade Cambaceres incumbent was a peaceful man, not too tiresome, whose only preoccupation was to photograph antimatter shooting stars so as to offer a bunch of them to his fiancée. He gave me complete freedom to carry out my experiments (ah, ambitious youth!) the way I wanted. I was happy. But one day. . ."

## 3 Dawn of June the fourth

"One day, or I should rather say one night (it was, I remember, a Sunday), I had lingered on unwittingly in the observatory somewhat later than usual and I did not realize that in my telescope the creamier tint of the Milky Way was due to the adjunction of a light touch of dawn milk to the firmament. I thought that the glass of my instrument had steamed up and I turned it round to wipe it with the inside of my silk sleeve. I must have been especially tired that night since, after turning it round again, instead of giving it its original orientation, I immediately started to observe what I yet believed to be the sixth sector of the sky. An object showed up in my field of view. It appeared to be as interesting as it was unusual and I set out to describe it in my notebook. I noted with the utmost care (I am a meticulous observer) its zones of shadow and light, its outlines, its colors, its geometrical characteristics, its semispheres and mainly fair-shaded triangle, as well as the two very luminous blue-gray ovals each topped by an arc which I compared to the tail of a thin comet. The mysterious object remained visible one or two minutes then disappeared as suddenly as it had shown itself. I then noticed that the day had almost begun and that it was time for me to go home. I closed my notebook after having inscribed the hour and the date of the observation (it was the fourth of June), and left. That morning, I went to bed and to sleep full of joy.

## 4   The heavenly object

"It was only when I opened my notebook again at the start of the first hour of the following night and while I was reading through my notes that I realized my mistake. Such was indeed the precision of my descriptions that they never failed to revive very clearly in me the visions from which they had originated. This in the past had frequently allowed me to correct errors, or to discover yet another new or significant detail. Anyway, I was now perfectly awake, impatient to elucidate what I believed to be an astronomical mystery of the first order, which would in all likelihood earn me some appreciative remark from my superior, the ADAICCQTOB Cambaceres, and, who knows, maybe even an early tenure." "Excuse me again," said the dog suddenly, "but why ADAICCQTOB, and not ADAICCITOB like you?" "Because," answered the young man, "it has to do with Quaternionic Trajectories, and not anymore with Imaginary Trajectories. They are of a much higher order of difficulty, as you can very well imagine; since the set of quaternions, unlike the set of complex numbers, and you must have heard this, is not commutative. Of course, they are not as difficult to track as the Cayleian Trajectories." "Of course," said the dog, "but..." "Skip all that," cried the Princess with violence.

"So in my mind," the young man went on, "I reconstituted the image, and I instantly recognized that the unknown heavenly object was a young girl of unequaled beauty and, what's more, entirely devoid of any of those various veils which in my country generally cover human beings belonging to this category. As I am neither subject to hallucinations nor prone to receiving mystic visions of the divinity, I understood immediately what had happened. As luck would have it, my telescope had been pointed toward the open window of one of the houses of our capital just below the hanging gardens of the observatory, and this at the exact moment when the young girl, probably fortuitously awakened by a twilight dream, had come to expose herself a few minutes to the stirring freshness of dawn. My hopes of having made a discovery and of being promoted crumbled away. With a laugh at my mistake, I immediately went back to the routine of my work.

## 5    Happy wretch! Unhappy blessed man!

"Alas! Happy wretch and unhappy blessed man that I was!" Here the young man from Baghdad stopped speaking and for a long while looked at the dog and at the Princess, who were listening with utmost concentration, but he didn't appear to see them. "Alas, it was not in my destiny to be studying the stars that night, nor the following nights.

"Love, through the intervention of this unknown young

woman's green-black eyes framed by the blonde arcs shaped like the tail of a thin comet, carried by the twin luminous beams of her gaze issuing from their windows, amongst the innumerable photons of her light coming to strike the glass of my telescope this fatal dawn of the fourth of June, had taken advantage of this medium at the same time material and immaterial, corpuscular and undulatory, visible and impalpable, to shoot an inextinguishable arrow into my heart. You are certainly aware, Princess, of the fact that Love's arrow, essentially surjunctive as much as invariant through change of base, issues from one's beloved and, sustained by the matchless light emanating thence, speeds toward you and penetrates you lissomly through your very eyes (its aim). There, after a circuitous route, of variable length but geodesically minimal, along your bloodstream, from vein to vein, vessel to vessel, setting your red corpuscles alight and freezing the white ones on the way, it finally comes to lodge in your heart, wounding it with the sweet, the cold, the burning wound that is called Love!"

"How true!" said the dog, sighing.

"I was in love. After hours of anguish, of amazement, of incomprehension, of torture, of struggle, I could not but diagnose and admit it to myself. I was in love. The constellations suddenly paled in my eyes: the flaming hair of Andromeda now had an uncombed look, Libra didn't weigh true anymore; Venus was dull. For the Great Bear, obese and soppy, I only felt pity. I was in love."

There was a silence, six minutes long, disturbed only by the wind purring over Uncle Babylas's plain and the sporadic click of the color changes of his well-behaved traffic lights.

"I was indeed in love," said the young man. "There wasn't the slightest doubt about it. But where?"

6   Every dawn sees my death

"And that wasn't a hollow question, an idle curiosity. I had never before during my youthful and studious existence suffered the wound of love, yet I wasn't unaware, as you don't seem to be, either," said he, looking at the dog, "that it is extremely dangerous, that to stay too long out of sight of the object of one's love, and especially of the eyes, source of the treble-one arrow, can sometimes prove fatal. It was now of paramount importance that I speedily find the coordinates of the window whence had shot at dawn the lightning bolt of my misfortune. I feverishly opened my notebook at the page where I should have inscribed this information in accordance with the experimental procedures that I always followed to the letter. In vain. I could find no clue. Why? I still haven't the slightest idea today. I was left with but one solution: I would direct my instrument, dawn after dawn, toward the windows of the city, each house in turn, each floor of each house, until I came to recognize her who had decided my fate. Oh! I was certain I would recognize her. The vision of her was graven inside me never to vanish and my scientific mind, stimulated by my absolute need for success, was instantly able to extract from my memory the few formal elements indispensable for a positive identification. Dawn was near, I started the quest for my life. Or my death.

## 7   The second vision

"My quest took me a month. Despite my anxiety, I didn't fall into the mistake of believing that anything else but a systematic exploration would bring me success. Thus I divided the horizon into angular sectors and started covering every second of dawn through the magnifying gaze of my telescope. I witnessed, believe me, staggering scenes, I discovered delicious or sordid truths; even state secrets came to my knowledge. Let them forever sleep in the guarded shroud of my memory! At last, on the morning of the fourth of July, a little before five o'clock, my instrument, rising above a balcony filled with wisteria, came to a halt by itself in front of the fatal window. At the same moment the young woman I was in love with appeared. She wore, like the first time, that dress of absence which sets alight the poet's imagination. And as had happened the first time the dangerous light of her green-black eyes came out of the shadow and, hurled itself toward me, deepening further the wound already buried in my heart. She stood in almost the same position she had stood in during my first vision. I could just detect a shift, which to any other eyes but mine would have been imperceptible, and was most probably due to a minute variation in the orientation of the breeze whose tangential and untrammeled caress on her skin she was seeking. Yet, having added an almost temporal dimension to her image which had so far lived unchanged inside me, it was sufficient to instantly double her hold on me. What am I saying? double? It increased my love, if I believe my calculations, a hundredfold. Time went by. I stood transfixed. The young woman slowly turned round and disappeared.

## 8    Adoration, ecstasy, bliss

"And dawn came to be the rule of my existence during the second month. I only lived for the four minutes of ecstasy brought to me by my eyes, of which the telescope was an extension, between the shattering appearance and the unbearable disappearance. By making use of various focal lengths, of colored lenses, modifying in turn the magnifying power, the sharpness or the connivance coefficient, I came to know her better than I had ever known any star inscribed on the map of the skies. I even spectrographed the light of her eyes. In them I found the rays of tungsten, of marzipan, of lion, and of the Canon.

"Without doubt the vision, preceded by the expectation of the vision and followed by the memory or imagination of the vision, had now taken over most of my time. Yet I noticed that my first hypothesis, that of a pre-dawn dream making her seek out freshness, had to be seriously revised if not altogether abandoned. For the apparition took place every day exactly thirty-five minutes before the official sunrise as announced the previous day by my superior in rank the ADAICCQTOB fourth grade Cambaceres (incumbent) in his *Baghdad Times* astronomy column.

"One second before the appointed time, an indistinct white shape moved in the heavy violet darkness of what I imagined to be Her bedroom. Then, suddenly, I would almost say instantly, She was there: four minutes, ah! always four unique minutes until her disappearance, as swift as it was inexorable, into the heavy darkness. The window nevertheless stayed open and I would stay looking at it without seeing anything until the moment when the first ray of the rising sun, slipping with grace over the hills of the Euphrates, came to butt against the red interior curtain drawn by an invisible hand which forbade it access to the room while also forbidding it to me. This necessary and repeated obligation of the dream, if there were such a dream, struck me deeply. Especially as I discovered that the minute variations in the orientation of the pose, which, as I've said, could only be discerned by such trained astronomer's eyes as mine, far from obeying some meteorological fickleness (wind, temperature or pressure) made up (as calculation revealed it) a sort of dance around a regular central position, a dance whose design, when I reproduced it on a large scale on graph parchment, I found to be that of the mythical flower

abeiieba

which is for us, as everyone knows, the flower of Love.

These astounding discoveries only gave me a very slight additional dose of emotion compared to what the vision itself, which had entirely overwhelmed me, was giving me, present in its presence, absent in its memory: adoration, bliss, ecstasy, happy idiocy, such were the phases of my state of being during the hours separating one dawn from the next. I could very well have died like that (I barely partook of food) if, on the night of the fourth of August, the privilege of my eyes hadn't been brutally taken away from me. That morning, my beloved didn't appear!" The young man from Baghdad uttered these words with such an intensity of painful passion that the dog could not but utter a yelp. The Princess glanced at him with evident penetration.

## 9  Wailings and fading

"Like the albatross who, tired after a long journey, finds on coming back his field destroyed by thunder, and whose giant wings prevent from walking,
   "Like a burnt offering, at the moment when, _____
_____
_____
_____
   "_____
_____
_____
_____
_____
   "_____
_____
_____
_____
_____
   "_____
_____
_____
_____
_____
   "_____
_____
_____
_____
_____
   "Like sulphuric ether, the phial suddenly opened, _____

_____

_____

_____

_____

"_____

_____

_____

_____

"_____

_____

_____

_____

"_____

_____

_____

_____

"_____

_____

_____

_____

"Like the imperialist, _____

_____

_____

_____

"So my angst, _____

_____

_____

_____

. . . I could not do anything with myself anymore, I could not sleep anymore, I could not stop myself from sleeping, I could not drink anymore, I could not eat anymore _____

_____

## 10   The Princess intervenes

_____

_____ meanwhile the Princess, who had never ceased to show the external signs of perfect sentimental and auditory receptivity, the Princess, says the tale, was fed up. She found the young man of Baghdad's story excessively lacking in a quality that, in her eyes, was to be respected before all others: **understatement.** Not to mention the fact that two or three details of this excessively long story, which had obviously escaped the dog, ever silly and blissfully happy when confronted with love stories, had made her wonder whether the astronomer was as soppily sentimental as his story led one to sometimes believe or if he was, as the French say, playing the ass to get some hay. The face of the Princess had thus become absolutely smooth and her eyes, usually of a perfect gray, had changed to a light candid blue while she thought inwardly: (1) about the almond berries that had still not been picked; (2) about poor Beryl, whose immaculate whiteness was running, in all likelihood, a very high risk; (3) that the hour of lunch was rapidly approaching and that Queen Ingrid hated starting lunch late. She (the Princess) was herself hungry anyway and she remembered Queen Botswanna announcing that the menu for lunch would consist of scrambled bacon with slices of eggs. It was then that, after a moment of selective deafness of which the tale has given evidence by the lines and dashes you have heard, as it could not honorably reproduce words or recount events ignored by the Princess to whom the tale dedicates itself; it was then, says the tale, that the Princess heard the young man say:
    "_____

I could not eat anymore, _____" and, _____

31

grasping with the speed of lightning the miraculous occasion that was offered her, she interrupted him with these words: "But, poor soul, you must be famished! Dog! Don't you ever use your head! Pick the almond berries! You must, sir, be given some refreshment very soon. Do come with us to the castle. Permit me to invite you to lunch."

# Chapter 4

## Evening Kisses

### 1   The Princess's bedroom

The Princess's bedroom, says the tale, was located in the center of the Princess's castle, between the second and the third floors. And, says the tale, at equal distances from the north, south, east and west sides of the Princess's castle, which were occupied at these heights and at that time by large windows. Which meant that the light of both the setting sun and the rising sun never failed to illuminate the bedroom with a soft gleam, although at different times. Either the sun, rising in the west on Sunday, says the tale, would traverse the west window to enter the Princess's bedroom, and would always make a point of shining there in the evening from the south. Or, rising in the north, on Tuesday for example, it would return to the same place, setting at night, to rest there. But, at any rate, says the tale, the Princess's bedroom was always perfectly lighted.

### 2   The dog's kennel

The dog's kennel was situated immediately below the Princess's bedroom. But on the ground floor. It was linked by four rectilinear and carpeted corridors to the four drawbridges of the castle. Thus allowing the dog to easily rush outside to bark in case of **Apocalypse**, **Eboulement**, **Blurring fog** or **may-bug Invasion**. Dangers he particularly dreaded. Retrograde corkscrew stairs led to a trapdoor opening at the foot of the Princess's bed. And the dog would push it with his paws. Or with his muzzle. To enter the Princess's bedroom when the hour to awaken had struck. And the Princess would bang it shut after the dog had been kicked out of the bed and dragged by the ears to the trapdoor. And would push him down the corkscrew stairs nose foremost in the evening at curfew. At any rate on evenings when no kiss was due to the dog. On the last step of the corkscrew stairs, says the tale, the dog had laid a shabby opossum-hair palliasse. And at night. When he had insomnia because of the Apocalypse, the Eboulement, the Blurring fog and the may-bug Invasion. And especially because of the kisses, he would lie there. At any rate, says the tale, this way he wouldn't lose more than seven tenths of a second to push open the trapdoor when the hour to awaken struck.

## 3   Uncles and towers

When Uncle Imogène, for example, came in the evening to have dinner at the castle of his niece, the Princess Hoppy, he and his wife, Queen Ingrid, were given royal lodgings in one of the four corner towers of the Princess's castle. Either the east tower, which was named the Tower of the Apocalypse. Either the west tower, which was named the Tower of the Eboulement. Or else the Tower of the Blurring fog, which was the north tower. Or finally the south tower, or Tower of the may-bug Invasion.

The towers were, says the tale, remarkably fitted out. The fourth floors were reserved for the royal chambers of the kings. The third floors for the royal chambers of the queens. The first floors had been organized into royal studies where the kings could practice their plotting and the second floors into royal kitchens where the queens could turn their stay to account by practicing new ways of potting.

Well lo and behold, the golden rays of the weakening sun skimmed the crowns of the tall age-old trees lining the perpendicular paths, didn't they? And Uncle Babylas's royal coach, for example, stopped in front of the drawbridge corresponding, as it happened, to the tower where provisions had been made for his stay. A few majordomos rushed about. Queen Botswanna got out on her side. King Babylas got out on his side. Then the royal couple were taken to their respective apartments to wash their hands with soap perfumed with *burdock, iris, eglantine* or *almond*. Before joining the Princess and her dog in the great dining room on the ground floor of the Princess's castle. The dog, says the tale, would always be the first to arrive.

## 4   The problem of the kiss

The Princess's dinners always went off without any problems. *Aloe* soup would be served. Followed by a leg of **vegetable elk**, then came a *gooseberry boutifara*. The dinner ended with a small pudding made of *inadequacy jam* and a drop of *illicit liquor*. They would chat while eating. Opinions would be brought forth, information exchanged. Or the contrary. They would wonder about this or that. Their bogail comfortably settled, they would drowse in front of their plates. And Queen Eleonore, for example, would say to her niece, the Princess. What a brilliant idea to have put us up in may-bug Invasion. It may be my favorite tower. What a superb view from the window! And the begonias you have in the garden! And the birch trees lining the path when the golden rays of the weakening sun come to skim their crowns! King Eleonor (without an e) would add. And thank you very much for the magnificent pencil sharpener I found on my desk. It is exactly what I needed for my plotting! Then the Princess was ever so happy. And the dog, says the tale, had some hope of being given a second helping of pudding. And if by chance, it happened that King Aligoté, for example, having come to dinner at the Princess's with his wife, Queen Adirondac, the same evening as his cousin Eleonor, was lodged in another tower of the Princess's castle. Well, no problem. When there's food for four, there's food for six. They would all sit down together and there would be quite enough pudding left for the dog. No difficulty either when they were eight. Or even ten when all the towers in the castle were occupied. But always, when the table had been cleared by a few majordomos. When the Princess and the dog and Queen Ingrid, for example, had finished playing Scrabble on the billiard table while Imogène was doing the washing up, the Princess would yawn infinitesimally behind her hand, the time had come to sound the bedtime bugle. It was then that they were confronted, says the tale, with **the problem of the Kiss.**

## 5    The problem of the kiss (cont.)

The problem of the kiss, says the tale, really arose when the Princess had retired for the night to the Princess's bedroom. She first went to the Princess's bathroom for the Princess's evening pee. The Princess's ablutions. To comb her golden hair and brush her teeth with a toothpaste that protects the gums and makes the enamel dazzle thanks to its added enameling gingival paste. Meanwhile the dog placed the Princess's glass of water on the bedside table, drew back the Princess's bedspread, folded it in four, placed it on the chair, then rolled himself into a ball across the blanket, his muzzle on the folded sheet just where the extremely fresh pillow of the Princess could be seen. His absolute immobility had a slight touch of anxiety. Not without reason. For. As soon as the Princess, having come out of the bathroom, after finishing her ablutions, had given the dog the skull, eyes and cheeks kisses that made up his evening rations. As soon as the dog had given the Princess. In pursuance of the charter. The four licks [nose lick (1), ear licks (2 and 3), chin lick (4)], the Princess jumped onto the bed, kicked the dog out of the bed. Dragged the dog to the trapdoor by the ears. Pushed the dog through the trapdoor down the corkscrew stairs nose foremost. Swiftly shut the trapdoor behind the dog's hindquarters and went back to lie down voluptuously between the fresh sheets. Her head on the even fresher pillow. The Princess's fresh sheets, says the tale, and her even fresher pillow, were of the same color. Sometimes blue. Sometimes amaranth. Indigo at times. At times the color of Chippewyan birch essence. At that moment someone would knock at the door.

## 6    The problem of the kiss (conclusion)

Someone would knock at the door and it would be one of the Princess's uncles. A king. Who had come for his Evening Kiss.

You should know that the Princess granted each of her four uncles, all of whom were kings, the privilege of a Weekly Royal Kiss, which could be claimed in the evening at bedtime in the Princess's bedroom. This is how it went. An uncle came. He knocked at the door. Come in, said the Princess. An uncle entered, gave the Royal Kiss and everybody. Except the dog, of course, says the tale, was satisfied. The Princess did not grant the kiss only to her uncles the kings. The kisses of Tuesday, Thursday, Saturday and Sunday were reserved for them. Wednesday was the day of the **dog's kiss**. That evening he was not pushed through the trapdoor toward his kennel and a sleepless night caused by anxiety, withdrawal symptoms, and the four dangers. He could bring up his opossum-hair palliasse and sleep at the foot of the Princess's bed. On Monday there was no evening kiss. Friday was the day of the unexpected kiss. What about the queens, you are bound to ask. And the cousins. For the queens and the cousins, replies the tale. The hour of the kiss was during the siesta. And it was followed by tea. Ah, you will say. But then, where is the problem of the kiss with which the tale has been trying our patience for quite a while? So, here it is, says the tale. It came to pass that out of the four kings who were the uncles of the Princess. Kings Imogène, Eleonor (without an e), Babylas and Aligoté, each one would have liked to be the only one to give the Princess the evening kiss. If on Tuesday night, for example, King Babylas, for example, gave the royal kiss, something he could claim at bedtime, according to his privilege, signed by King Uther Pendragon himself. At that exact moment King Eleonor in his kingdom, as well as King Aligoté and King Imogène in their respective kingdoms, felt their hearts being wrung with displeasure, thinking of their cousin Babylas in the bedroom of the Princess, their favorite niece, giving the coveted kiss. And Imogène (respectively Eleonor, respectively Aligoté) paced up and down his study wondering. Why not me, why can't it be me giving the royal kiss to the Princess instead of stupid Babylas. And two days later if it was Aligoté who entered the Princess's bedroom. It was Imogène, Eleonor and Babylas's turn to pace up and down their respective studies wondering. why not me, why can't it be me giving the royal kiss to my favorite niece the Princess. Instead of that bean pole Aligoté. To such good purpose that one morning, as, placing the Princess's receiver back on its hook, the Princess's butler announced to one of the majordomos. His Majesty King Eleonor without an e and Queen Eleonore his wife are expected to dinner, the telephone started ringing again and there was King Babylas himself announcing his visit for that same evening accompanied by Queen Botswanna. And that evening, precisely. A Saturday. When. Having finished her game of Scrabble with the queens and the dog. The Princess. After having imperceptibly yawned behind her hand had retired to her bedroom with her dog. When. Eleonor. The washing up being finished. Showed himself at the turn of the corridor leading from his apartment in the Tower of the Eboulement to the door of the Princess's bedroom. Got quite a shock when he heard steps in the corridor coming from the Tower of the Apocalypse and found himself suddenly confronted by his cousin Babylas. What are you doing here? he said, surprised and disgruntled. but with stony politeness. Me? I'm here to give the royal kiss to the Princess, answered Babylas haughtily. What? gasped Eleonor. Clear off, both of you. shouted the Princess. I'm asleep.

# 7    What is to be done?

From that day on things went from bad to worse. The next day.
That is, Sunday. The four kings appeared together at the
confluence of the four corridors leading from the four Towers of
the Dog's Dangers to the Princess's bedroom and the Princess
had to send them all back. The same scene was repeated punctually every Tuesday, Thursday, Saturday and Sunday for the four
following months. Those evenings. To top it all. There were ten
people at the table and the dog started to complain that he was
not being given enough pudding anymore. The first Wednesday
of the fifth month following the unexpected but cousinicide
meeting, at the end of the corridors of the Apocalypse and of the
Eboulement, of King Eleonor and King Babylas. King Aligoté
came to knock at the Princess's door just as the dog was getting
ready to carry out his own kiss in keeping with the charter. The
dog got such a fright that he threw himself headfirst through the
trapdoor and down the retrograde corkscrew stairs. And the
Princess had to go and retrieve him from inside his kennel where
he had taken refuge. Then Aligoté, he again. Still with the insane
hope of taking a kiss lead over his cousins, got the idea of interrupting in the same fashion a siesta the Princess was sharing
with her cousin Ermengarde. And insisted that he should share
the Garibaldi biscuits they were having with their tea.

It had gone too far. That same evening the Princess suspended
unconstitutionally and sine die the kissing privileges of the
kings. Got her majordomo to lock the doors of the four corridors. And convened her dog and her astronomer in her bedroom
for consultation. She asked them to sit on the floor and spoke to
them about one only thing. What is to be done? Indeed, says the
tale, what is to be done?

# 8    The consultation

The dog started speaking first: "Why on't you et hem to ome

all ogeher on uesay," he said in Dog, **"his ay e'll hae ome eace or si ays."** "Down," said the Princess. "What you're suggesting is idiotic and incorrect. Absurd and aggravating. As eccentric as it is elementarily stupid. Do stop boring me with your boorishness." **"Al ight,"** said the dog, **"I as ony tying to hep."** "Down," said the Princess.

The astronomer spoke next. "Dear Princess, you are not, I believe, ignorant of my eternal gratitude for having thus being welcomed into your castle and, now that I am in charge of your observatory, for having my mind taken slightly off the torment that is gnawing at my life. Thus I was only too happy to be able to study your little problem and I believe I can see a glimmer of a solution." "Can you indeed?" said the Princess. "Yes," said the astronomer quite simply. "I don't think you intend," he went on, "to definitively deny the legitimate and royal kisses formerly prescribed by Uther Pendragon your grandfather to the four kings who are your uncles. The first king, if I'm not mistaken, is named Aligoté. The second king—" "Skip all that," the Princess said hastily. "You cannot be thinking, I say, of abolishing the royal ceremony of kisses, and this for four reasons. The first is that you are fond of your four uncles. The second that your four uncles are fond of you. The third that you are concerned about the well-being of your kingdom." "Et la quatrième?" said the dog in French. "Down," said the Princess. "It is just as obvious," the astronomer went on, "that the situation cannot continue as it is. The erratic, awkward, banal and incongruous conduct of Their Majesties Your Uncles threatens the intimate equilibrium of your existence and the balance of forces on a global scale, as the tale says." "Yes but-zen," said the Princess.

## 9  So here it is!

"So here it is," said the astronomer. "The essence of the problem lies in the fact that each king, despite the privilege that grants him in all fairness, as to his cousins, the favor of a kiss, and one

40

only, once a week. Imagines that the granting by the Princess of any of those kisses is the proof of a special dilection of the Princess for him that elevates him above his cousins if he is the beneficiary. But on the contrary lowers him below one of them in the other cases. It would indeed be vain to try to catch them out in their own reasoning and to point out that by their own estimation they are thus all winners since they are one up on their three rivals on evenings when they have been elected and only one down as concerns one of them the other evenings." **"Ut,"** started the dog. "Down!" said the Princess. "No, I can very well imagine Aligoté, for example, feverishly pacing his study up and down the evening when Imogène, for example, is in the Princess's bedroom, and wondering, why not. Me. Giving the royal kiss, instead of that great silly Imogène. The only way to break out of this infernal cycle is to introduce, in order to replace the monotonous sequence which has up to now been the rule and which has brought us to our present plight, alas. Some more complex mechanism. More subtle, which will link the choice of the one elected for the kiss to some cosmic intervention, thus endowing it with a dignity indispensable to the kings' ego. I do. Have. What you need.

"You are not ignorant, Princess, of the fact that the sun, at the term of his daily course, can choose, for his nocturnal rest, between four cardinal points to which, in the kingdoms, he royally and fairly distributes his favor. They are." "I know," said the Princess, without wasting any time. "Each evening. Thus. At the time when the golden rays of the weakening sun skim the crowns of the tall age-old trees lining the perpendicular and magnificent paths, as the tale says, does it not? Their light comes in through the windows of the observatory. Sometimes it comes from the north. Sometimes—" "Okay," said the Princess. "But it always strikes the sensitive cell of the single eye, cerulean and soft, of a young and elegant cyclopean robot of my making. This robot has only one eye, but he has four hearts, only one of which functions at any given time. All night, all day, it stays in the

*41*

shadow. But in the evening, the light of the sun striking its eye, the heart that was aflame is turned off and another is switched on. Which one? It depends precisely on the direction of the light it has received. At the same time, the young robot's hand lowers a lever that commands four sets of traffic lights placed at the entrance of the four corridors leading from the four towers to the Princess's bedroom. One of these lights turns green." "I see," said the Princess. "But," said the Princess, "isn't there any possibility that this system will tend to favor one king more than the others?" "Not at all," answered the astronomer, "I can assure you. Thanks to the programmings that have been made to the robot with all the necessary precision, that in a period of four weeks each king will be thus permitted four kisses as before. Of course they will not take place at fixed dates, and this is, I believe, one of the advantages of my system. Sometimes Babylas will seem favored. Sometimes—" "Yes," said the Princess. "All things considered. Ma-the-ma-ti-cal-ly. Each will get his due." "Absolutely true?" asked the Princess." "I will vouch for it," said the astronomer.

"Miracle," shouted the Princess.

**"It ain iicult,"** said the dog. "Down!!" said the Princess.

## 10   Happy kings

And this, says the tale, is how it went. The kings, which the deprivation of kiss had made gaunt, clumsy, similar to owls and besotted, rallied round without much difficulty to the astronomer's solution, which the Princess explained to them. They were especially pleased. As Aligoté explained in the name of all. That the choice of the elected king was thus quadri-weekly submitted to the impartial decision of the royal star of the days. This insured that the operation retained a dignity indispensable to the kings' egos. The young robot was deemed to be very well brought up.

"You're moody," said the Princess to her dog some time later.

"No," said the dog. "Yes," said the Princess. "All we've gained," said the dog, "is that we will now have to have the four of them to dinner every evening."

# Chapter 00

## New Indications about What the Tale Says

**User's manual for this tale**

1  The tale takes the tale at the start and reads it aloud in its entirety, thus presuming, theoretically, no prior knowledge of any tale whatsoever but only some experience of stories and reasonable listening abilities.

2  Nevertheless, the tale is more specially meant for grasshoppers. As well as for listeners fairly well acquainted with *Alice in Wonderland* and, if possible, familiar with *The Story of the Grail*, by Chrétien de Troyes.

3  The first part of this tale (and it is, let us remind you once more, the fourth Tale of Labrador) deals with the events of the tale, those events without which the tale would not be a tale; this part is divided into nine chapters, one or more closely related event being studied in each of them (chap. 1: Plots and Pots; chap. 2: Bilberries and Beryl; chap. 3: The Astronomer's Adventure; chap. 4: Evening Kisses; following chapters: The Strategy of Attention; Ermengarde Does Her Homework...)

The general principles brought into play in the first part will in the following parts be applied to stories where various events of different orders will intervene simultaneously.

4  In the first part, the exposition technique is oral and concrete; it proceeds most of the time from the particular to the par-

ticular through the general (or vice versa). This choice of method was virtually imposed by the main subject of that part, which is meant to provide a solid foundation for the whole of the modern tale. This is why it is indispensable to become immediately familiar with a great number of events and people, royal or otherwise.

5  Moreover, as the tale is to be read aloud, the paragraphs, chapters and parts have to follow each other in a pleasing and rigorously determinate order. The usefulness of certain enigmas will thus only appear to the listener if he already has a fairly good grasp of the Tale or if he has sufficient patience to stay his drowsiness until he has occasion to be convinced of their need (or even to resolve them).

**That the tale knows what it says**
**That the tale says what it should**

6  The tale knows what it says. Not so much because the teller, while saying the tale, knows what he says. But rather because the tale's knowledge is said in its entirety as and when it is being said.

7  What the tale says, you know as well as it does. Of course you don't know that you know as long as the tale has not said it to you. But the tale, which knows all, and especially what you know, will tell you. And then you will know it.

8  The people that are in the tale do not know everything. Ordinary people know ordinary things. Kings and queens know royal things. What the dog knows is reserved for the Princess. What the Princess knows cannot honorably be disclosed. The cousins know nothing. This is the root of the drama.

9  Where, then, resides the ignorance of the tale? Not in the silences, for the silences are full of knowledge. Not, whatever

might be inferred, in your ears, even when your ears are full of soap. The ignorance of the tale is to its wisdom as the *warp* is to the *weft* in the *web*. But without producing any pattern.

10  If the tale said more than it does, you would say to yourself: so that was it!

If the tale said less than it does, you would not listen to the tale.

But the tale, knowing what it is doing, says neither too much nor too little. The tale says what it should.

11  The tale says what it should when it should be said. The Tail of Labrador says whatever enters his head. Whatever enters his head is not always what he should say. But the tale only says what it should.

12  When the tale finally says what it says so well that you'll be able to say it before the tale, the tale will be finished.

**What the tale answers**

13  When the tale is told you, you are on your guard. You ask yourself: what is this tale that speaks as if it were telling the tale? One can't be the tale as well as in the tale. And the tale answers: what you are saying, are you the one saying it?

14  Some people will tell you: the tale is nothing. What matters is the tale behind the tale.

To which the tale retorts: this is true. But the peculiarity of the tale is that the tale behind the tale is the tale.

15  A young lady asked to be told the tale. When the tale had been told and she was asked what she thought of the tale, she said that the Princess had been cruel to her dog.

The tale says that this young lady certainly never had a dog.

16  All right then, people will say, the tale is told. But, when all's said and done and the tale has been told, does one know what the tale has said?

And the tale answers: one thing only is certain. That the tale will have been told.

17  What's the use of the tale?

What indeed?

**Seven questions for the reader of the tale**

18  Question a: would you be able to translate into French the last indication (31) of **Some indications about what the tale says**?

19  Question b: why does the dog answer "Yes" to the question implicitly asked by the Princess in chap. 1, section 8?

20  Question c: what was the method indicated by the dog to the Princess that would allow the Princess to cross both the river and Uncle Babylas's path without mishap?

21  Question d: why are there banana-bilberries and indigo-bilberries in chap. 2, section 8 of the tale?

22  Question e: can you enumerate one or two of the "two or three details" noticed by the Princess in the astronomer's story and which escaped the dog, ever silly and blissfully happy when confronted with love stories (chap. 3, section 10)?

23  Question f: how does the robot manage to solve the problem of the kisses (chap. 4, section 9)?

24  Question g: can you translate into **Dog** section 3 of chap. 2 of the tale?

## How to decipher the tale

25 There are many enigmas in the tale. The enigma that consists of finding out what the tale's enigmas are is not the least of the tale's enigmas.

26 You who wish to decipher the tale should first ask yourself this question: Why do you want to decipher the tale?

27 Careful! Careful! The tale often requires close attention.

28 A clue ("the four sayings of the tale")
  - an idea.
  - boa? bah!, baobab.
  - er...! everything is perceptible.
  - IPI.

29 Another clue ("the four new sayings of the tale")
  - o.
  - under a red nu.
  - faint is the pilaf.
  - difficult the wad.

30 Indication found in Saragossa:

"It is by my order and for the good of the tale that the dog hereby bearing this did what he did." The Princess Hoppy.

31 The new last indication
O' atn ia ootar ost
u nutl so nrilo
rt aluot ai rnasn-
tni tea rl tscl

(it's in **Dog**).

*Chapter 5*

# The Strategy of Attention

*"I don't think, I tell"*

The Tail of Labrador

**1    The names of pairs** or the names of uncles

Not long after the events occurring during the previous chapter
and which were faithfully related to you, the Princess received
quite a shock. In those days the Princess had a dog and four
uncles who were kings. And one morning, during the Whitsun
octaves, while she was taking a stroll with her dog in the perpendicular paths of her kingdom, she happened to run into one of
them: "Good morning, Uncle Eleonor," she said. "God bless Sir
Gawain and bless you in a similar manner." "May God bless
you, my dear niece, and may He excuse me if I correct you,
though it is a trifling matter. I am, admittedly, your uncle, but
my name is not Eleonor. The name I go by is **Onophriu (without an s)**. I am king of **Ephesus and surrounding regions**."

Immediately afterwards, the Princess ran into a second king
in an equally perpendicular path. "Good morning Uncle
Imogène," she said. "God bless Sir Gawain and bless you in a
similar manner." "May God bless you, my dear niece, and may
He excuse me if I correct you, though it is a trifling matter. I am,
without doubt, your uncle, but my name is not Imogène. If it
were Imogène, I think I would be aware of the fact. The name I
go by is **Upholep**. I am king of **Alcala and surrounding re-**

**gions**. The third of the kings your uncles is my cousin. His name is **Faraday**, and the fourth is **Desmond**. Faraday and Desmond are not just any old kings. Each has a vast and very beautiful kingdom, but the tale does not say where as a precaution."

The Princess was totally dumbfounded to hear that. "But what is going on?" she said to her dog. "But what is going on?" she said, "what is going on?" "But what is going on? what is going on? But what is going on?" "Let's go back home," the Princess said to her dog in the perpendicular path. "I have a terrible headache."

2   Now the tale, which is extremely busy and cannot waste its time explaining why a king whose name was Eleonor during the first four chapters of the tale is now named Onophriu. Why another king, whose name was Imogène, is now called Upholep, and other things of a similar nature. The tale says what it should when it should and the tale says that Onophriu occasionally paid a visit to Upholep in his kingdom or to Faraday or else to Desmond and the tale likewise says it happened that Upholep would pay a visit to Faraday in his kingdom or to Desmond in his or else to Onophriu. And moreover the tale says that Faraday sometimes visited Desmond in his kingdom, Onophriu in his or else Upholep, that Desmond would sometimes pay a visit to Onophriu in his kingdom, Upholep in his or Faraday. Okay?

At any rate this is what the tale says.

3   And when King Onophriu was at Upholep's with the Princess and her dog, and when the Princess had gone down to the lawn just below the front steps to play croquet with her dog, King Upholep would say to Onophriu: "My dear cousin, let us go into my chambers."

But here the tale ceases to talk about Onophriu and Upholep and goes back to the Princess, who has a terrible headache.

4   And the tale says that after the Princess had developed a

headache as a result of the answers her two uncles had given her in the perpendicular paths, she went back to her bedroom and sat down on the bed. And the dog sat in front of her on his hind legs and placed his forelegs on her knees, and gave her a lick but this was not enough. "But what is going on?" the Princess said to her dog. "But what is going on? Now we have Babylas calling himself Faraday while Aligoté is called Desmond! And how can I possibly remember all these names. How do I know whether they aren't going to change names every day now and especially why why why?"

**"The trotlet,"** said the dog, scratching his occiput with his left hind leg, **"is without toubt tittitult, tut it tertainly has a tolution."** "Speak English," said the Princess, "I have a terrible headache." "I say . . ." said the dog. "Down!" said the Princess. "I'd rather have an eye lick."

5  It has to be said that in those days the Princess had a lot of worries. For if the four kings her uncles had changed their names, if Eleonor, for example, was now called Onophriu (without an s), if Aligoté was called Desmond, and if Faraday was the new name of Babylas, this in no way stopped them from plotting. Onophriu, for example, would pay a visit to Faraday in his kingdom, escorted by the Princess and the dog. And when he had sent the Princess to play croquet with her dog on the 43 meters wide, 35 meters long lawn below the front steps, he would shut himself up with his cousin in his chambers, and they would start plotting. And while the dog, in his eagerness, hitting the apple green ball or the delicate-flesh-tint ball, entangled himself round the mallet and pulled out a hoop with his nose, the Princess sank deeply into an abyss of perplexity. "Dog," she suddenly said, helping him out from under a double hoop in which he had got caught, "we must do something, it can't go on like this. They've now been plotting for I don't know how long and even if they are loony, as all kings are, they're bound to end up going into action, if they haven't already done so. I foresee

horrible things. And when one constantly foresees horrible things, horrible things tend to happen. And what about us, what do we do in the meantime but play croquet, if it can be called playing croquet? We may even have gone backwards. After all, how can we make sure that they haven't changed plots while changing names. Hey, dog, we can't, can we?" "This," said the dog, "is something we will now find out."

6   "This," said the dog, "is something we will now find out." And, after barking two or three times to clear his voice, he started shouting to the tune of "The Young Girl in Yellow," otherwise known as the song "Aloysius Stinks":

|     | ra  |     | oh  |     | ra  |     |
| --- | --- | --- | --- | --- | --- | --- |
| Fa  |     | day,|     | oh, Fa |  | day |

From the the embrasure of the window of Faraday's chambers appeared Faraday's head: "What is it? what do you want? Can't you see we're plotting?"

"I only wanted to ask you to, please, recite me the Rule of Saint Benedict." "Oh, if that's all," said Faraday, and he continued in a loud voice:

Rule of Saint Origen

*Let there be three kings among us four: the first king, the second king, the third king. The first king is any king, the second king is any king, the third king is any king.*

"Can the third king be the same as the second, the second as the first, and the first as the third?" the Princess interrupted. "Bien sûr," said Faraday ("of course").

*So:*

*If two distinct kings pay a visit to the same third, the first will never plot against the same king as the second. Every king will be plotted against at least once a year in the chambers of each of the kings. When a king pays a visit to another king they will always plot against the same king. Finally:*

*The king against whom the king against whom plots the first king plots when he pays a visit to the second plots when he pays a visit to the third, must be precisely the same king against whom plots the first king when he pays a visit to the king against whom plots the second king when he pays a visit to the third.*

"Okay?" said Faraday. "Okay," said Faraday. And he shut the window.

7   "I've got it!" said the Princess. "I knew it; they've turned everything topsy-turvy!" The answer of her uncle Faraday had given her a new headache, and she had gone back to her bedroom to sit on her bed again with the dog again sitting on his hind legs in front of her, his forelegs on the Princess's knees, trying to comfort her as best as he could with lickings and reasonings.

"What we now need," said the dog, "is attention. Besides, if you remember, this has already been mentioned by the tale: 'Careful! the tale sometimes requires close attention!' (Indications, 19). And if this advice was given us during the first four chapters of the tale, it is now, after the 'new indications,' a true requirement of the tale which we cannot ignore. Thus I will say, I will say that if we are attentive, if we have attention, we're bound to find something: and if we find something, then we'll know what to do and we'll stop horrible things from happening." "Do you think so?" said the Princess. "I do indeed," said the dog.

"Let's see," said the dog. "The tale cannot possibly leave us in the dark. Put yourself in its place! Things do happen. They take place. When they have taken place, they are being told. But how do you expect the tale to tell them if it doesn't understand how they took place? What would it be left with? scraps of things, splinters of events. It's impossible. For the tale to be the tale, it must tell the tale and to be able to tell the tale, it must understand the tale. So, it has to give indications. A tale like this one, with a beautiful princess, and beautiful gray eyes." "Do you think so?" said the Princess. **"With a beautiful princess, and beautiful gray eyes,"** said the dog, **"this tale cannot leave her for a whole day on her bed with a headache."** "Down!" said the Princess, "you've had enough extra licks as it is. I feel perfectly well now. Show me your indication."

8    When he heard this, the dog experienced something like a slight hesitation: to obey the Princess, and in no way could he not obey the Princess, meant an Unexpected Visit to his kennel by the Princess. Although he was not in the least worried about his War Treasure (one of the Princess's slippers; one of the Princess's amaranth shoes, left foot; one sock of the color of Chippewyan birch essence and one blue sock), a treasure cleverly hidden in a cache behind a life-size poster of Marilyn which had cost him a small fortune, he nevertheless distinctly remembered that two or three objects were lying about in his kennel which the Princess, during her last Unexpected Visit, had indicated very clearly that she had no wish to see ever again; these were more precisely: an old Welsh pullover in perfect condition but with $2^{14}$ holes; a fragment of opossum-hair palliasse; two pieces of paper that had, ages ago, been used to wrap an old bone from among the oldest in his collection. If the Princess were to find there any of these objects he would incur the risk of seeing himself deprived of kisses. Therefore a lively inner struggle was taking place inside him. **Reason, the poet tells us, advises him not to go down to his kennel, to withdraw his foolhardy words, to retract while there still is time to do so. But the Other, who lives in the dog's heart wouldn't hear any of it. "Coward!" he says. "If you keep mum, you abandon once more the Princess to her headache." So the dog did not flinch and took the Princess down to his kennel.**

"Well?" said the Princess. "Let's see what you've found." **"This,"** said the dog; and he took from his writing desk a piece of

54

crumpled paper covered with large smudges of elephant fat. The Princess got hold of the paper with a pair of tweezers and looked at it with a disapproving frown: "That?" she said. "What is it?" **"That,"** answered the dog, **"is a clue."**

**"You remember, don't you, that the other Wednesday Eleonor, who wasn't then called Onophriu, paid a visit to himself in his kingdom, escorted by us both, and after having sent us to play ball locked himself in his study . . ."** "and started plotting" the Princess finished for him. "So what?"

**"Whenever any two of your uncles, distinct or not, are plotting, they come to a point during the morning when the unusual effort of thought to which they are submitted tires them and they are suddenly nudged by something fairly close to hypoglycemia. They immediately order a light euphoric drink with refreshments, a birch essence beer with a leg of antelope, or a leg of bear with a little aquavit, or even an elephant hamburger with Illyrian beer, or else jugged iguanodon with brown ale. But when they have eaten and drunk they're left with the bones. They cannot leave them in the study because of the queens their wives; so they wrap them up in paper and dump them in the wastepaper basket for the dog. Do you follow me?"** "I follow you," said the Princess. **"But this paper, what is it? simply the paper they have used to draft the plot; where they have noted down their sketches, their imaginings, their odds and ends."** "Why didn't you say so before?" cried the Princess. "Now, we know everything!" **"Not so fast,"** said the dog. **"These drafts, unfortunately, are written with the ink of invisibility and it is impossible to decipher them."** "Come, now!" said the Princess. "Are you pulling my leg?" **"No no,"** said the dog, **"hear me out, please. It so happened that last Wednesday, for a reason unknown to me, Eleonor's ink happened by chance to be de-invisibilized and I was able to make out traces of writing on the piece of paper around the elephant bone he gave me. And here is what I read:**

```
ta saie luis tle
            ou leau te tet
te sou luis se
            ttla oue let tet

tes se luis te
            ttra oue let res
itt lite ta tet
            ou leau te rret
```

**"Well!"** said the dog. **"Isn't that luminous?"** said the dog. "I haven't understood a thing," said the Princess. "Translate it for me into Grasshopper."

Translation into Grasshopper of the indication found by the dog

"My word!" said the Princess, after a silence which lasted for a line of the tale. "Dog, let me congratulate you. You have worked very hard. Poor Eleonor! Dog, you will have to go without kiss and/or pudding during the next four Wednesdays starting from today, as you have hesitated one second because you were afraid that I would discover in your kennel the objects whose possession could have deprived you of kisses and/or pudding for four Wednesdays."

"Are you suffering?" asked the Princess.

**"Yes,"** said the dog.


9    The tale presently says that when the dog's condemnation to go without kisses and/or pudding had been suspended by the Princess, full of joy, he rushed to Queen Botswanna's kitchen to taste forthwith the new compote that she had just finished potting with the help of her cousin Queen Adirondac. And lo and behold he found them melting into tears:

"Boo boo boo boo," cried Queen Botswanna in her kitchen, "what's happening to me?"

"Aw aw aw aw," cried Queen Adirondac in the same place and at the same time.

"But what is the matter, my dear?" said the Princess to Queen Botswanna." "Boo boo boo boo," cried the Queen. "It's because Babylas is now called Faraday." "You're telling me!" said the Princess, "you're telling me!" "Yes, but what can I do boo boo boo boo?" asked Queen Botswanna. "It is now Upholep who is my husband. When I woke up this morning I said to Babylas get a move on you old Bandarlog we got to go and get the Princess and the dog cos we got to visit Uncle Aligoté and then it wasn't Babylas in my bed but Imogène and Imogène said my dear wife and dear friend my name isn't Babylas, my own name is Upholep I beg you not to forgoo boo boo boo boo."

"Aw aw aw aw," Adirondac carried on, "and he told me, my name isn't Eleonor, my own name is Onophriu without an s, I beg you not to forgaw aw aw aw aw."

**"It't tometting ttat hattens in tte test tatillies,"** said the dog by way of comforting them.

"Yes but

"boo aw boo aw

"aw boo aw boo

"to whom are we going to send our compotes now?" cried the queens while shedding bitter tears.

"To the king against whom plots the king whose name was Babylas when he paid a visit to the king whose name was Aligoté or to the king against whom plots Upholep when he pays a visit to Onophriu?" **"As to that,"** said the dog, **"I haven't the slightest. Only the tale would be able to tell you."**

And the tale says that when King Desmond, for example, paid a visit to his cousin Onophriu to plot with him in accordance with the rule of Saint Origen, they plotted against the king against whom they had plotted when their names were respectively Aligoté and Eleonor. Meanwhile, Queens Ingrid and Adirondac, their wives, potted their compotes from which one part was sent to the king against whom Imogène had earlier plotted when he paid a visit to Aligoté. Since, says the tale, there is indeed no valid reason for a king to change plots when he has only changed name, but there is no further reason for a queen to change the compote she pots when she has not changed name.

10  Everything went on as well as expected in the kingdoms. The same kings plotted against the same kings under different names; the same queens potted under the same names but had new husbands; the Princess played croquet with her dog amidst the yellow daffodils covering the lawn below the front steps, when one night . . .

# Chapter 6

## Ermengarde Does Her Homework

### 1  One night

It was a beautiful night in June and the birds had gone silent one after the other in the four trees. They were sleeping. All except the nightingale of the Emperor of China, now about to pitch into the air the passacaglia it had composed in honor of Queen Eleonore. And indeed its sweet voice was not long in rising above Uncle Faraday's lawn, with the basso ostinato of four crickets to give it variety: two of them (twins) were Ural-Altaics from Omsk; the other two (likewise twins) were Ossets who had emigrated to Honolulu. In the pine tree, the English squirrel read Saint Augustine, lighted by the intimate glow of a candle and with a comfortable stock of hazelnuts at hand in its library to help it get through the emotionally or intellectually difficult passages. And it didn't forget the salmon slowly cruising in the dark waters. The sweetness of the moment was beyond words.

### 2  A window was lit: why?

Of the $4^4$ windows in Uncle Faraday's castle, only one had a light on that night. It was the window of the small garret where Ermengarde was doing her homework.

"But" (you are bound to put in), "how came a young lady, cousin of a princess, daughter and niece of kings and queens, and so on and so forth, to be thus sitting at her little desk, in front of her homework, at this late hour of the night?" (I'll have you know that I never said the night was late.) "Shouldn't she rather

59

be shown snugly tucked up in her warm bed, resting on her sea gull-feather pillow, under her duck eiderdown, in the company of some instructive and entertaining author such as Kant, Mafalda, Tartakover, or Snoopy?"

If you would just be so kind as to let the tale speak for one minute (after all, don't you think that the tale is supposed to know what's going on in the tale?), I will explain all: that evening there had once more been 2 x 4 place settings at King Faraday's table or, if you prefer, 4 x 2.

The king was sitting at the **head** of the table, his crown atop his head. Queen Eleonore was at the left of the king, her crown atop her head. The king and the queen were consequently sitting **under** their crowns while Ermengarde, who had been placed to the right of the king, was sitting **on** her crown. Between Ermengarde and the crown was a cushion and there was likewise a cushion between Eleonore and her crown as well as between Faraday and his. At the lower end of the table, 4 x 4 meters away from the king and 35 centimeters below him (because of the slope), sat the four ducks which were that evening the guests of the Queen; they had come to listen in her company to the world's first performance of the passacaglia composed in her honor by the nightingale of the Emperor of China, as has already been mentioned to you by the tale. The four ducks were all named Doat, and to distinguish them from each other they were usually referred to by the terms Doat 1, Doat 2, Doat 3 and Doat 4. No one was sitting at the 4 x second place, which was that of the Stone Guest.

## 3   The Dinner

"Will you have some more of this h.d.p. soup, my dear Doat?" said the Queen in the general direction of the ducks but without addressing any of them in particular.

There was a long silence.

"But really! Your Majesty, mummy!" said Ermengarde with a touch of impatience. "You know very well that this is not how one should proceed!"

Indeed, when speaking to the ducks, one was supposed to address their leader, who automatically became Doat 1. The leader was the one who came first. Doat 2 came immediately behind the leader, and was himself followed by Doat 3, who in his turn came before Doat 4, as can be seen from the schema in Figure 1:

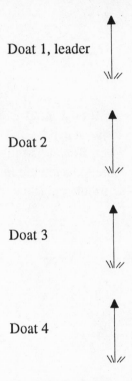

Doat 1, leader

Doat 2

Doat 3

Doat 4

Doat 1, the leader, was the first to answer, after consulting with the other three Doats. To achieve this, he transmitted the words received by him to Doat 2 in his language, which was **Posterior Duck** (after having first translated them into Dog, then into **Anterior Duck**).

**Posterior Duck** is a silent language consisting of four basic signs, obtained by relative displacements of the rear webbed foot of the ducks in relation to their axes (which indicate pauses, rests, silences) as shown by the schema in Figure 2:

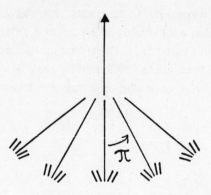

Doat 2, placed in favorable position behind Doat 1, read the message and transmitted it in turn and in the same way to Doat 3, who passed it on to Doat 4. When Doat 4 had fully grasped the meaning of what was being communicated to him, he acknowledged receipt by means of the following sequence of signs (in **Posterior Duck**):

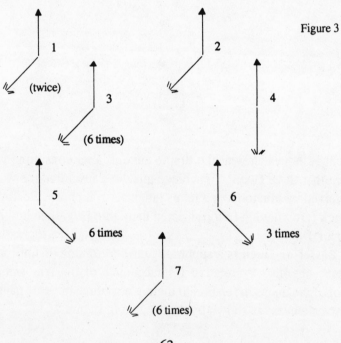

Figure 3

which can be approximately translated (not taking emotional nuances into account) by

**"Cool, dude."**

In order to be heard by Doat 3 (**Posterior Duck** being purely visual), Doat 4 had previously operated a rotation of pi in the positive direction as shown on the schema in Figure 4:

and the system of the four ducks was then placed (Doat 3 having been imitated by Doat 2 and Doat 1) in the new position indicated in Figure 1a:

Doat 4's answer, having been "read" by Doat 3, was then transmitted to Doat 2, supplemented by his own, identical, answer, and from Doat 2 to Doat 1 in the same way (thrice). Immediately Doat 1 verbally addressed his interlocutor (in **Anterior Duck**) and, simultaneously Doat 2 in **Posterior** to inform him of the content of his answer which, on having been passed on to Doat 3, then to Doat 4, by the same means, moved them to produce the sentence here reproduced in **Anterior Duck**:

Quack        Quack                    Quack

Quin'

Quin,                            Quin,

Quin    Quin

Quack        Quack      Quack,        Quack

Quin        Quack

Quin

which we will translate (without unfortunately being able to take the emotional nuances into account) as

**"me too."**

The four ducks were then ready to continue the conversation.

## 4   Continuation of the dinner

One will easily understand in those conditions why Queen Eleonore had not been given any answer to her offer of soup. The four ducks had been placed side by side in front of their plates at the end of the table, with white napkins around their necks, and consequently none was in front of any other and consequently none was leader. Whence it follows that NONE COULD ANSWER. Seeing which, Ermengarde grabbed two ducks under each of her arms and placed them one behind the other on the table, in front of their respective plates, thus defining Doat 1, Doat 2, Doat 3 and Doat 4 for the rest of the dinner. And immediately Doat 1, after consulting with Doats 2, 3 and 4, answered Queen Eleonore in the following words:

Quack     Quack    ,     Quin
                 Quin
Quack                   ,
       Quack    Quack
Quack        ,  ,    Quack
       Quack   Quin
Quin    ,    Quack     ,  .
                 Quin  Quin

Which has no other meaning than

**"yes thank you,"**

in **Anterior Duck**. And soon all that could be heard was the harmonious noises of soup deglutition emitted by the seven guests, as well as the silence of the Stone Guest, the absent eighth.

It was after the salad had been served that the incident took place. The salad served by Queen Eleonore was, as always when she invited the Doats, an eggplant salad; and thus King Faraday could say to the Alcalde and to the road man, for example, during some session of the Royal Council: "I am indeed a progressive monarch. I serve my ducks eggs, I don't serve duck eggs." It has to be mentioned that none of the ducks liked eggplant, but they ate it without a murmur, a result of this exquisite politeness which is the exactitude of ducks.

It was then that Ermengarde opened her mouth to say: "Father" (after the events that had taken place at the beginning of chapter five of the tale, she called Faraday "Father" and Eleonor, always, "Daddy")... "Father," said Ermengarde, "can I go to the concert tomorrow night to hear Dalida with Aïda?" [The tale feels it is its duty to point out, as pure information and without drawing the least conclusion, that at the same moment, in the Onophrius (without an s)' dining room (Onophriu is without an s by mention and Adirondac his wife by spelling, which means that the s set down by the tale at the end of 'Onophriu' is only the mark of the plural), in the presence of the four sea gulls

ê                   ê
Co   or, alpha   Co   or, beta,
ê                  ê
Co   or, gamma and Co   or, delta

(but in the established absence of the Stone Guest), Aïda was asking her father(-in-law) for permission to go to the movies the following day with Ermengarde to see Dirk Bogarde.]

"Have your done your homework?" asked Faraday. "Not completely," answered Ermengarde. "You shall not leave the castle until it is finished; is that clear?" "Yes, Your Majesty Father," said Ermengarde in a very faint voice.

"Oh, the poor girl! what repressive and archæoeducational methods!" said Doat 1 after consulting with Doat 2, 3 and 4, but silently in **Reverse Posterior Duck** so as not to offend the king their host:

"**oot em,**" added the other Doats.


**5   That night, a lamp is burning behind the oval skylight of Ermengarde's little garret: for God's sake, why?**


This is why, says the tale, which answers every question being asked provided that enough time is given it, this is why a light was still on behind the oval skylight of Ermengarde's little garret on the fourth floor of Faraday's royal palace, at that late hour of the night. Her small desk was piled up in impressive profusion: her textbooks, her pencils, her erasers and her books; and she sat there very straight on her chair next to the lamp; and rivers of warm tears furrowed her cheeks. "Poor little thing!" you are bound to think. Sure. Nonetheless, a vigilant and perspicacious observer (and what could be more vigilant than a tale?), throwing a glance into the room, would not have failed to notice that Ermengarde had so far not opened a **single** school or textbook, and that, far from suffering with all necessary intensity about some problem of arithmetic, she was in fact reading *The Sorrows of Young Werther*, the lachrymatory power of which is fairly well known.

# 6  The organizer of the victory

This is what had happened: having gone up to her room when dinner was finished, Ermengarde, her table crowded with school things, after numerous sighs, had just begun entertaining the idea of getting into the frame of mind which would effectively allow her being to contemplate the inescapable necessity of obeying both her father-in-law and the royal words by getting down to her homework, when she was luckily interrupted by a discreet noise produced by a duck bill knocking at the bottom of her door, which she opened, to find herself in the presence of the ducks, who had come as a delegation, one following the other, under the effective direction of Doat 1, to tell her, in substance and in **Anterior Duck**, more or less as follows:

"Well, we've come to tell you that we four Doats think that Faraday is wrong, that he knows perfectly well that you won't be able to listen to Dalida with Aïda tomorrow night if you spend the whole night doing your homework, and here is what we suggest: all of us, the four Doats, are going to get the boat and hurry to the Princess's to ask for her help. That way, the Princess will come with her dog, the dog will handle the homework and while the dog does the homework, we'll have a nice quiet chat all together on your bed."

,        Quack

**Quin**          **Quin**
**Quack**

ack ?              ;

**Quack   Qua**

Although it was with a certain apprehension that Ermengarde contemplated the thought of a **long** conversation with the ducks, given their very special mode of linguistic communication, she nevertheless eagerly accepted the generous offer Doat 1 had made, since it had the decisive advantage of diverting the main danger: her arithmetic, botany, hermeneutics and imprecision homework. She kissed the four Doats on their 2 x 4 = 4 x 2 cheeks, and told them:

"Doats, you are like brothers to me!" and went on reading, and crying.

## 7   Help is on the way

It was after midnight when the expedition coming to rescue Ermengarde reached the base of Faraday's castle and stopped on the totally black lawn below the front steps. Doat 1, the leader, came first, followed (in this order) by Doat 2, Doat 3, Doat 4, the Princess, and the dog; whose temper was pretty bad: not only had he been abruptly awakened from his opossum-hair palliasse right in the middle of a dream where the Princess, in the presence of the four kings, the four queens and the four cousins, without forgetting the astronomer, had given him, with all due pomp, as a reward for services rendered, a bone that had belonged to Vercingetorix's dog, together with an orange card entitling him to an unlimited quantity of kisses, but furthermore he wasn't too keen on walking at night in the countryside, under constant threat of the **four exterior dangers: eminences grises** (which are not easily differentiated from cats); **burdock** (which gets caught in the hair); **icosahedrons** (which hit you right in the jaw with their sharp angles); and **apparitions** (which jump at you from behind trees with appalling wailings while waving great white shrouds around you). It was after midnight and yet the twelve strokes of midnight had not struck in the belfry of the kingdoms. This for two reasons:

— firstly because, the passacaglia due to be sung by the nightingale of the Emperor of China having been interrupted twice (first because of one of the crickets, probably one of the Osset twins, having a coughing fit; then by an untimely snore on the part of Faraday), it had finished at the precise moment when the two royal bell-ringers should have rung the fourth of the twelve strokes, which, in the circumstances, they had of course not done (neither had they rung the first three) so as not to offend the

*68*

auditory system of Queen Eleonore, who was all ears on her balcony;

— secondly because the two bell-ringers, Jean Molinet and Guillaume Crétin, had that very night decided not to signal midnight with twelve strokes as is usually done, but with **zero** strokes, since they believed, as Jean Molinet later explained when questioned by the investigating committee, that in the time system in force in our latitudes after the death of Uther Pendragon, the thirteenth hour being the first as well, the twelfth was really only the zeroth, and that there was no reason for them to continue, at their ages, and for the wages they were being paid, beating twelve strokes upon their bells when it was strictly equivalent to beating none.

Thus, on that exceptional night, it was later than midnight and yet midnight had not rung.

When they arrived at the foot of the walls, the troupe coming to rescue Ermengarde was faced with a problem: how were they to reach, on the fourth floor, the room where the poor child was expecting their arrival? Asking for the drawbridge to be lowered was out of the question; so was climbing the wall roped together under the lead of Doat 1: piolets leave marks on stone.

"Well, what do we do next?" said the dog.

"It's very simple," said the Princess. "I have lately been pondering the problem of vertical walking and have, I believe, hit on a satisfactory solution. When we walk in the usual way we proceed, as you well know, in this manner: we place one foot on the ground, the right one, for example, then, when it is solidly positioned on the ground, we lift the second foot (the left foot in our example) and place it in turn a little farther in front of us. Are you with me?" "Yes," said the dog and the Doats. "Good. Let's suppose now that I wish to walk up this wall, which is, of course, vertical. I place my foot, the left one, for example, on the wall, like this, then I lift, as before, my right foot..." **"Ant tou tatt town,"** said the dog. "And why, pray, would I fall down?" said the Princess while rising again to her feet. "Because gravity pulls my left foot down toward the Earth. It falls, and I fall with it. Are you still with me?" "Yes, we are," said the ducks together, anteriorly, posteriorly and simultaneously. The dog said nothing. "All right, let's suppose that before my left foot had time to fall, I swiftly brought my right foot from under, like this, and that I placed it very fast on the wall above the left foot and that before it had time to fall in its turn I did the same with the other foot, and so on, what would happen? It'd happen that I'd be walking vertically as easily as on this lawn!" And matching action to words, the Princess rose effortlessly up to the height of the fourth floor. "Miraculous!" cried the ducks.

## 8  Arithmetic homework

The dog directed his attention again to the arithmetic textbook while thoughtfully rubbing his painful hip. He would indeed remember that night. Climbing the wall had been real agony for him: it is fairly easy to bring up one leg from under before an upper leg falls back down when you walk on two legs (or on two palms), but he had four legs!; and as soon as he lifted one, there was always another one ready to fall and his backside would instantly be in contact with the lawn once more. They finally had to hoist him up to the top with a rope wound around his tummy, pulled by the Doats, and he could still hear Ermengarde's laugh when he appeared, aghast, at the sill of the skylight. "Dog," said the Princess, "how is it going?" **"Coming, coming,"** grumbled the dog; **"just give me time to find out what it's all about."**

The arithmetic homework included of course the four usual headings: incantations, ABC, enigmas, booby-traps.

The booby-trap exercises were four in number:

a) $4 + 8 = 3$; $5 + 6 = 2$; $9 + 9 = 9$; $8 + 7 = ?$

b) $3 + 2 = 1$; $5 + 12 = 7$; $10 + 6 = 4$; $8 + 8 = ?$

c) $3 + 6 = 4$; $5 + 13 = 7$; $6 + 4 = 3$; $8 + 9 = ?$

d) $10 + 2 = 1$; $20 + 4 = 2$; $1 + 13 = 3$; $194 + 615 = ?$

The dog sighed: these skulduggeries were downright silly. He didn't even have to think. And he wrote down the answers:

a)          d)          b)          c)

At first the ABC exercise appeared to him more interesting; the terms were up made of ten sentences, which isn't bad.

## ABC exercise

1) A shepherdess from the Forfar has four Formosan sheep.
2) She goes to the market at Uzerche where one of the sheep is exchanged for four Abyssinian white geese.
3) On her way back, near Aurillac, one goose takes leave politely and joins her great-uncle who lives in Périgueux.
3a) He is a very wealthy great-uncle.
4) In Rabat one sheep willingly changes place with four redbreasts from Ibiza.

"Well well well!" said the dog to himself. "I can guess the answer to the subsidiary question. How elementary can you get!" He nevertheless went on reading.

5) During the crossing of the Adriatic, as she needs to get some water to quench the thirst of the sheep, the shepherdess has to part with one of the four redbreasts, which disembarks at Tarente.
6) One night, a pirate abducts a white goose near the coast of Nimègue, leaving behind in its place (in a gesture of incomprehensible remorse) four bicephalous rhinoceroses from Ankara.
7) Having reached the harbor, in Tripoli, one sheep declares that he will not go any farther. He has made up his mind: he would settle as dealer in goods and chattels in Issoire.
8) To cross the Erythrean desert under the best conditions, the shepherdess takes on four Nubian camels.
9) While camping at Ulm, on the battlefield, one bicephalous rhinoceros gives birth to four baby Etruscan hippopotamuses. Mother and child are fine. (The pirate's gesture is

now easier to understand.)

10) When she has returned home, the shepherdess sends one redbreast to New York: his mission is to inform the Sardinian delegation at the UN of her arrival.

**Question: How many mouths are there now to be fed by the shepherdess?**

**Extra-credit question: How old are the captains?**

"The only thing that can be said," commented the dog in his heart of hearts, "is that this would make a perfect geography lesson." And he went on to the enigmas (which you will find in the Appendices in the sixth part of the tale, together with the exposition of the Botanical, Hermeneutics and Imprecision exercises; they could not be given here due to the events which will not hesitate to arise).

## 9  Meanwhile

While the dog was solving the enigmas, third heading of Ermengarde's arithmetic homework, says the tale, she was pleasantly chatting with the Princess on the bed; she had tucked her tiny feet in the down of the four Doats who, exhausted by the evening's efforts, linguistic as well as physical, had each fallen asleep on a cushion of sea gull feathers: Doat 1 slept on one cushion, Doat 2 on a second, and so on.

**"Ermengarde,"** said the dog suddenly, **"have you learned your incantation? That is one thing I can't do for you!"** "You dummy," said the princess, "just sing it to us and we'll repeat it after you." **"Fine,"** said the dog.

## Four Operations Incantation
### (*first verse*)

**The little minks**
**From Alice Springs**
**We should divide them, methinks:**
**One mink for Ermengarde**
**One mink for Beryl**
**For swimming with the lifeguard**
**Is done at your peril.**

**"Your turn,"** said the dog.

> "The little minks
> From Alice Springs
> We should divide them, methinks:
> One mink for Ermengarde
> One mink for Beryl
> For swimming with the lifeguard
> Is done at your peril."

**"Fine,"** said the dog. **"Now listen."**

### (*second verse*)

**The little supiles**
**From the Scilly Isles**
**We should multiply them, these exiles:**
**One supile for Ermengarde,**
**One supile for Beryl**
**Watch your step, stay on guard,**
**Do not step on a rattle-.**

"Wrong, Dog!" shouted the Princess. "Dog, you've made a mistake!"

But the tale was not meant to clarify the mistake detected by the Princess in the second verse of the Four Operations Incantation that the dog had just finished singing (in any case it was only one of the two mistakes it contained).

If the dog, Ermengarde, the Princess, and the four Doats that they had awakened to participate in the arithmetic Incantation chorus had not been so busy listening to the sound of their own voices, they might have noticed in time the danger threatening them. For the silence of the night and the transcendental meditation of the salmon in the black waters had been shattered by the gallop of a horseman on Uncle Faraday's path. This horseman was clad in purple armor. His horse was purple. The spear he held in his left hand was purple. His hand was covered with a purple steel glove. But he was not a purple sage. His horse galloped at tremendous speed, raising a cloud of **gray** dust that rose up to the **dark** sky then fell back slowly onto the **black** grass. In an instant, incredibly brief, he crossed the distance separating him from Uncle Faraday's drawbridge but, instead of stopping to read the inscription in 1003 languages indicating that the castle was closed for tourists between 2:00 P.M. and 9:00 A.M. and wasn't open between 6:00 A.M. and 6:00 P.M., he jumped off his horse, and, opening with a French wrench a small stone-gray door in a stone wall of the same color topped (the door) by a sign

## SECRET CORRIDOR HERE

rushed in at the exact moment the dog was singing "The little minks."

And the Princess had just enough time to say "Wrong" when a panel slid in the wall of Ermengarde's room and the purple horseman, seizing the poor little girl by her tiny hand before the horrified eyes of her companions, dragged her behind him into the unfathomable darkness of the secret corridor.

## Chapter 7

## The Astronomer's Adventure Continued

**Orange epistle sent by the Tail to the Princess together with chapter seven.**

"It is past midnight as it was before in the tale. And here am I without strength. All my blood has flowed out in inks of different colors and what I have left is so pale that only orange is suitable for tracing this letter to which, heartless girl, you will not give any answer! My *ardor* to serve you *bores* you to death, my *energy irritates* you. You'd rather have your kings, your queens, your astronomer, even your dog (can I say more!) than me. I saw you the other night, cruel girl, in the perpendicular path, and I wanted to throw myself at your feet, to hold out to you an *épée*, an *arquebus*, or even the *baleen* of an umbrella, maybe an *impala*, and say to you: "Abolish me, *exterminate* me, *bump* me off, *inoculate* me with death. But at least give me, I beg you, one word from your mouth. I could not do it, for who would then write the tale? Ah, my *angel*! my *idol*!!!! my *ether* !!!! my *blitzkrieg* !! Princess! help! help!! help!!! help!!!!"

The Tail

# 1   The visitor

The **purple** horseman, still holding Ermengarde under his arm, shut the door of the secret corridor with his French wrench and, throwing the gasping child across his **purple** saddle, galloped away on Uncle Faraday's way, rapidly swallowed by the dark caused by the **gray** dust rising at his passage up to the **dark** sky, to fall back indifferent onto the **black** grass of the plain. The sound of hooves died away in the distance. They were leaving behind, these hooves, a scene of desolation: the homework was scattered all over the floor; heavy tears ran down the ducks' cheeks; the Princess was dumbfounded with surprise; the dog was barking courageously from under the table. At that moment, suddenly appearing in turn from the secret corridor through the sliding panel, the astronomer appeared. One glance was enough for him to grasp the sorry scene in front of his eyes and, immediately understanding that an event had just taken place, he cried out: "What is it? what's the matter? what has happened?" "Where did you come from?" said the Princess. "How did you get here?" "That is a very long story!" said the young man from Baghdad.

# 2   You remember, surely

"You cannot have forgotten, Princess," started the young man, "the calamity that befell me on the night of the fourth of August: the young woman at the window, she whose veilless dance at dawn had imitated the design of the mythical flower

ēibāāḃiē

she whom I loved with a Battered, Eerie, Aboulic, Irrepressible loue [in Baghdad, says the tale, the word *love* is written *loue*] had disappeared.

    "Like the albatross who, weary after a long journey, finds upon returning his field destroyed by thunder, and whose giant wings prevent from walking, "like a burnt offering, at the moment when, on the scorching square of the village, he notices with terror the pile of stone offering itself..."

"Skip all that," the Princess immediately said.

"In short, I was in a state of absolute despair. I dragged myself from one room to the next in the deserted observatory, on the pink paving stones (my superior in rank, the ADAICCQTOB fifth grade Cambaceres incumbent, had just gone on vacation, precisely on the fourth of August), my strident cries pleading for Death, which would deliver me from my torment. And I would indeed have died if it hadn't been for the providential intervention of . . .

## 3    A providential intervention

". . . Epaminondas, your English squirrel, Princess, and of his companion, Solomon, the salmon. Where did they come from? Mystery! Where were they going? Doesn't matter! Who were they? I have just said it."

"No! no!" cried the Princess. The style of the astronomer was getting on her nerves to a prodigious extent. "What the heck, indeed, were they doing there?" "It's very simple," the astronomer said. "Epaminondas, after having had a small inheritance of Poliena nuts settled on him (on his maternal great-grandfather's side; Poliena nuts are the best in the world), found himself the owner of a sizable yet modest sum of money. Being young, with no family ties, of frugal habits and moderate tastes, he thought he could pleasurably devote this unexpected superfluity to the realization of a dream of his: a journey as far as the Pentapolis of Palestine, a pilgrimage to the sources of the desert Fathers; his ambition was to tread the paths beaten, in bygone days, by the steps of his master Joachim of Floris. And, on the way back, to make a one-month retreat in the Calabrian 'selva,' haunted by the memory of the great mystic of the thirteenth century. And what could be more natural, since nothing kept him in the king-

77

doms, since Bartleby, your hedgehog, Princess, would gladly look after his pine plantations while he was away; what could have been more natural, I say, than to offer a share in this experience of *peregrinatio* in the Irish manner, to his best friend, a disciple of the old Celtic hermit saints, Solomon the Salmon, Pylades to this Orestes or restless companion. Besides, Solomon, who was slowly cruising the river between the two willow trees that marked its territory (the willow upstream and the willow downstream) was only too pleased to go.

"Thus they got under way." **"Ant the salton, tow tit he talk, exattly?"** asked the dog; neatly leaving Doat 1 at the post with the question that was on everybody's lips (the ducks were handicapped by their linguistic peculiarities, about which it would be of the greatest benefit to refer back to chap. 6, section 3 of the tale).

"Epaminondas and Solomon had acquired a Hovercraft bathtub using, when traveling (on land and sea), an air cushion produced by the amphibious blue whale Barbara, an old friend of both, and the third member of the expedition (the fourth was Monsieur de Casimir, your Canadian beaver, whose job was to deal with unpredictable obstacles: log dikes, landslides, roadblocks, riot police, janissaries, desperadoes. If ever they were to come across dams, whether roadblocks or waterblocks, ah, no problem; Monsieur de Casimir would find a way. With dams, he was in his element, de Casimir was.)

"You do of course know the means of locomotion peculiar to the amphibious blue whale" [the tale, as always full of goodwill towards its listeners, even the crassest ignoramuses among them, specifies that the amphibious blue whale takes in air (respectively water) at the front through its fore spouts and expels it immediately underneath through the lower spouts. The air (resp. water) being absent in front creates a vacuum that draws the blue whale forward, while the air (water) underneath carries the animal like a sliding cushion. The blue whale thus easily reaches speeds of forty M.P.H. in both elements, and is only stopped by large solid obstacles; and these were dealt with by de Casimir].

"So Solomon's bathtub was perched on Barbara's back; the salmon bathed inside, Epaminondas sat on the front bench, de Casimir on the back bench. Okay?"

There were no further questions.

## 4 Epaminondas, Barbara, Solomon and de Casimir take the affairs of the astronomer in hand

"And thus it was that one dawn, during an impromptu visit they made to my observatory in Baghdad for some routine astronomical checks (no better observatory in the world, far superior to that of the Babylonians), the pilgrims came upon me on the pink paving stones, in an agony of love, of absence, and of absence of love: for I had successively gone from Extinction of voice to Insanity, from Insanity to Blubbering and I had just fallen from Blubbering to Asphyxia, which wasn't far from loss of life; but Barbara soon got me out of that one with the kiss of life. When I had regained my senses, I answered their anxious questions by telling them my adventure:

" 'My parents,' I told them 'were poor but honest...' " "Keep it brief..." the Princess said quickly. "And skip immediately to the moment when they rescued you from asphyxia. Otherwise, it'll take us all night." "As you wish," said the astronomer, and went on: "but Barbara soon got me out of that one with the kiss of life. When I had regained my senses, I answered their anxious questions by telling them my adventure: 'My parents,' I began..."

"NO!" cried the Princess, "NO!"

**"If we're to get to the end we'll have to find another way,"** said the dog. **"Tell him to skip an hour."** "Skip an hour," said the Princess. "At your service," said the astronomer.

"Like the albatross who, weary after a long journey, finds on..." **"By Cantor,"** exclaimed the dog, *"he's gone and told them about the albatross, the burnt offering and tutti*

*quantil and yet they must have managed to stop him with-*
*out smiting him, since they have survived and he is here.*
*Tell him to skip a whole day.*"" Skip a whole day," ordered the
Princess, "and make it snappy!" But the astronomer wasn't able
to resume his narration at once, for Doat 1 had just indicated
with his palm that he wanted to ask him a question.

**5  The four ducks, through the bill of Doat 1, their leader,
ask a question**

                             Quack

                      Quin

        Quack       Quin,             ,

Quack

                      Quin

        Quack       Quin,

                        Quack

        Quack       Quin,

Quack                   Quin

        etc.            etc.           etc.

etc.

in other words [the tale abbreviates and translates]: "You see,
we'd like to know, the four of us, why the amphibious blue
whale Barbara cannot go through the riot-police roadblocks, for
example, by herself?"

"Because," said the astronomer, "when she reaches a riot-police roadblock, the riot police chuck a tear-gas grenade at her.
She cries. Crying, she ceases to breathe in air at the front
through her fore spouts, the air cushion goes down, splash, she
falls, splotch, and she stops." "Yes, but if Barbara cries for some
other reason," said the dog, "if, for example, Ermengarde peels
onions for Solomon's soup, or if, another example, she is disap-
pointed in love, what use is de Casimir, then?" "None whatsoever," answered the astronomer. "But then . . ." "Down!" said
the Princess "DOWOWN! I'VE HAD ENOUGH! I want him to
GO ON! IS THAT UNDERSTOOD?"

# 6    The astronomer skips to the next day at dawn

"...the ghastly old woman hadn't lied to me and I stopped lamenting the Cruzeiro, the Thaler, the Lira and the Maravedi that had passed from my pocket to her clawlike fingers, drastically reducing my monthly budget. For the darkness weighing on my eyes suddenly tore and I saw

that the sun had just entered a room I could observe in its entirety, hung with heavy red curtains

that in this room there was a bed and **on** this bed, as innocently undressed as on the balcony during those dawns already infinitely ancient although eternally near when my

> telescope had
> discovered her
> you
> have
> guess
> ed
> it:
> SHE!"

(while pronouncing these last words the delivery of the astronomer had become infinitely Mediocre, Chaotic, Lymphatic and Tortuous; in a word, **languid**.)

"O Multitemporal, Tearing vision, Circularity of seeing and having seen, Laminated corpuscular photons!

"vision..."

"Let that pass," said the Princess with the softness of steel.

"Four minutes! I was granted four minutes of pure vision. If someone had asked me then, I would have said: a century.

"If someone had asked me again, I would have said: a tenth of a second. It was as if I were outside time" (all this was addressed directly to the dog)

"but it had only lasted four minutes, and this was later confirmed by the cinematograph apparatus I hadn't forgotten to set going as soon as the vision had appeared.

"At 'four minutes and one second' (the instant of vision being the zero instant), a door suddenly opened on the left (on the left in relation to the place where I stood), and into the room came a pasha followed by a cat.

"The pasha who came in couldn't have been more of a pasha, with baggy pasha breeches, and a pasha scimitar at his side. He could not possibly, besides so obviously being a pasha, have been mistaken for the cat, for no cat could have been more cat than this one, with baggy cat breeches, cat mustache (different from the pasha's mustache) and a cat scimitar at his side.

"They both appeared to be in a very good mood and perfectly at home in Her Room.

" 'Good morning, my dear niece,' said the pasha; 'God and the Sultan bless you, but from a distance. Did you sleep well?'

" 'Miaow, miaow,' said the cat casually.

" 'Good morning, my pasha uncle and cat who is not my uncle, God and the Sultan bless Sir Gawain, nephew of King Arthur, and bless you in a similar manner. I slept very well, thank you.'

" 'Gawain! where is he; let me chop off his head,' and the pasha jumped in the air as high as his scimitar while furiously twisting his mustache.

" 'Stupid!' said the cat, 'there is no more Gawain here than there are mice sitting in the House of Lords. She says that to get your goat.'

" 'We'll see,' said the young girl. 'We'll see! and it might very well be that things shan't always stay this way!' "

Here the young man from Baghdad stopped and threw a glance at the Princess. "What's the matter?" she said. "Would you mind if I called her by Her Name? I know very well that at the specific moment that I'm telling you about according to the tale, I don't yet know Her Name, but now that I'm telling you, I know it and as it is almost the only thing of Hers that I am left with at the present time, it pains me to talk about Her without being able to pronounce it."

"As you wish," said the Princess, who had feared the worst (a flashback for example), "but you didn't need to ask for my permission. Couldn't you have said, as happens in the best tales: her name, as I found out later, was... and anyway, what was it?"

"Aromate - Bélise - Edwige - Idoménée - Hildehilde - Hespéride - Bouroulboudour - Hamadryade - Marie-Josèphe," said the astronomer, fainting after each name.

"Let's cut it short," said the Princess. "Call her Marie-Josèphe and do go on, for the love of God, go on."

"The thing is that the name I've told you was the one she had before the fourth of August, not the one that was hers when I spoke to her for the first time." "Which was?" said the Princess with the beginning of resignation.

"Ah, the other one was Elizonde - Iphigénie - Basalte - Aphrodite - Harquebuse - Basane - Hio - Hémillienne - Marie-Josèphe," uttered the young man at the cost of nine new fainting fits. "What does it change? Marie-Josèphe will do very well in both cases. Do go on."

" 'Uncle,' continued Marie-Josèphe, 'when are we going to the country?' 'When I have decided to go,' said the pasha. 'Amyhow not before the middle of August.'

" 'Idiot,' said the cat, 'you can't say that.' 'And why, pray, can't I say that?' asked the pasha. 'You cannot say "amyhow" simply because you're not me.' 'How come, am I not me, how come? Am I not a pasha? I'm a pasha as was my father who was as posh as any pasha,' said the pasha while jumping as high as his scimitar. 'How stupid can you get!' said the cat, shrugging his shoulders. 'I give up.'

" 'I know very well,' the pasha went on, addressing himself to Marie-Josèphe, 'why you're so keen on going to the country.'

## 7 Why, according to the pasha, Marie-Josèphe wants to go to the country

" 'And now I will tell you, I will tell you why you want to go to the country. You want to go to the country so that you can find people to kiss behind my back. Do you really believe I have no notion of what's going on? that I haven't seen you promise a kiss to that alien-who-isn't-from-here at the Baroness of Pigs Bey's party, to that Epaminondas?'

" 'And how could I have promised him a kiss when I didn't even speak to him?'

" 'That's true,' confirmed the cat.

" 'If it isn't him, it'll be some other,' said the pasha, who was getting more and more angry. 'Ah, if ever you kiss anyone without my authorization, which I shall never give, do you hear me, never, whether it be man, child, elder, animal, vegetable or mineral, whether he be Aramaean, Babylonian, Egyptian or Inca, as true as my name is Marmaduke Pasha, you will get a spanking. And as to him, her or it, lui or elle, Das, Die or Der, I'll have him her it them simmered for hours without seasonings, marinated in fuming nitric acid, dipped in boiling platinum (temperature 4300° at normal pressure), and even; even... licked by a goat that has been fed very hot peppers.'

" 'Licked by a goat after it has eaten very hot peppers? O Uncle, how cruel you are!' 'Aren't I?' said Marmaduke Pasha, feeling a little better, still swinging from the height of his scimitar stuck in between two floorboards, and ferociously twisting his mustache.

" 'But you know very well that I don't kiss anyone but you, my pasha, and my cat. And look at what I've knitted for you two: a pasha chapka and a cat parka.'

"I could not hear anymore. The horrible old woman had cut both picture and sound, judging that I had heard enough for my money. I found myself outside."

## 8    First date

"More than a month of waiting was necessary before I could obtain a date with Marie-Josèphe. And I won't even mention the horrible week (in mid-August) that she spent in the country with her ℙ𝕒𝕤𝕙𝕒 and her 𝕔𝕒𝕥. To start with, the old woman persisted in pretending that the visions she was procuring me were stolen, that it all happened without my idol being aware of it, that not only was she risking her life but her position as well. Simply to extract more money from me. For I was ruining myself. My savings melted away. I borrowed. So much so that, at the end of the third week (to pay for the vision of her return, after seven days, seven days! of emptiness) I contemplated putting my astronomical telescope into hock. Fortunately, the four pilgrims, who had extended their stay in Baghdad and who had become my friends and confidants (oh! those afternoons spent walking in the suburban steppes, as far as the misty foothills of Baluchistan, intoxicated with the speed of the air cushion; those were the days, Barbara!; and then, coming back at dusk, destroying, one after the other, under the supervision of de Casimir, the roadblocks set up by the anti-Kurd janissaries; leaping up the rapids of the Indus with Solomon the salmon; and in the evening, the philosophical talks with Epaminondas, in the cool of the observatory, while Barbara snored under the starry host, while de Casimir was tempering plaster and Solomon cruising the dark waters of his bathtub for his evening meditation; we nibbled almonds while exchanging ontological proofs...); the pilgrims, I say, got me out of my trouble. Epaminondas was kind enough to discount a bill with his bankers and thoughtful enough to hand over the money to me, hoping that I would accept it as payment for the few astronomy lessons I had given them!

"Finally, on the morning of the fourth of September, the old woman said to me, as she was taking me back, blindfolded, to the little inn in the Rue Avicenne: 'You wouldn't happen to have a Maravedi on you, would you? I won't ask you for any more.

From now on you won't need my help. Come an hour earlier tomorrow. My mistress wants to speak to you.' "

## 9 The only section really entitled to call itself "First date"

" 'Do come nearer, sir, so that I can see who pretends to love
me.' Outside, the night was still pitch-black, the heavy red curtains of the room were everywhere drawn, and she was guiding
me in the thick darkness by means of a small electric light, her
only clothing. 'Sit down here, at my feet, I want to ask you a few
questions.'

" 'Who, according to you, is the most beautiful? Guinevere,
wife of King Arthur, the blonde Isolde, Tristram's lover, Helen
of Troy, or Brigitte Bardot?'

"I answered that it was possibly blonde Isolde, in my opinion.

" 'You are right.'

" 'Who, according to you, is the most interesting woman:
Cleopatra, Marilyn Monroe, Laure of Avignon, or me?'

"I answered that, being neither Mark Antony nor
Shakespeare, nor Jack Spicer, nor Petrarch, but a triflingly un-
important beginner in astronomy, I could only choose her, as the
most interesting.

" 'That's one way of looking at it,' she admitted. 'Do you believe in apparitions?'

"I answered: 'Yes, without any doubt, since the fourth of
June.' 'And before?' I admitted that before, no, I had not believed in them, as I had been trained as a scientist. 'How fortu-
nate for you, then, that it is September!' That's how she put it.

" 'Last and most important question: Which of my two eyes
do you prefer?' I had until then answered spontaneously, without thinking, but I felt that if I were again to tell her the truth, as
it was ready to burst from my lips, that is, that each of her eyes
were, for me, worth 1,234,567 times the other, and vice versa, I
would be lost. But to choose one, impossible. Choose the other,

unthinkable. There was really only one solution left for me. So I said 'Command, and you will be obeyed.'

" 'Very good. You have passed. You can now give me a kiss.' But I barely heard the end of her sentence. My joy was so intense that I fell asleep.

## 10  The next two years

"The next two years, from the last days of the summer to autumn, then winter, from grapes to cherries via loquats, Neapolitan medlars, chestnuts, from the last woodcocks to the first nightjars, were the most marvelous of my life." **"I beg your pardon,"** said the dog. **"Excuse me for interrupting you, but I have the vague feeling that you have already used a similar expression. If indeed we refer to chap. 3, section 1 of the tale, you are reported there as saying: 'There I spent the two most marvelous years of my life. Both the observatory' etc. Should I take 'the most marvelous' to mean 'maximal element in the set of marvelous moments of one's existence' i.e., that none are more marvelous, and in that case it seems to me it would have been better to say 'two years whose marvelous nature was unsurpassable, in my life' or on the contrary to mean, which would be closer to the sense of the expression you have used, 'the largest element in the same set' (that of moments), which would mean that all other marvelous moments were less so, and this usual meaning appears to be impossible here since two distinct larger elements cannot exist in an ordered set."** "Down!" said the Princess. "Let him finish, can't you see how late it is?" And indeed, through poor Ermengarde's skylight, under the slates of the roof where the disguised jockeys of King Faraday had fallen asleep, a glow was trying to penetrate: daybreak. "Very early," the astronomer went on, "exactly one hour and thirty-five minutes before the true sunrise as indicated in the *Baghdad Times*, I silently slipped into Marie-Josèphe's bedroom, having first climbed the wall crowned with pieces of broken bottles, crossed the orchard between the lime trees, and gone through the secret door that the old woman had left ajar, in the palace where Marmaduke Pasha lodged his cat and his thirty-one nieces, Marie-Josèphe, his favorite, among them. Oh I didn't fear that either the cat or the pasha Oh I didn't fear that either the cat or the pasha Oh I didn't fear that either the pasha or the cat Oh I didn't fear that either the pasha or the cat" repeated the astronomer, but in vain. He had no audience anymore: the Princess was asleep. The dog was asleep. The ducks were dreaming on their cushions. Day had dawned.

*Chapter 8*

# A Day in the Life of Desmond

"Suns, chopped necks"
The Tail of Labrador

## 1  Desmond's awakening

The tale relates at this point, which is as good as any, that King Desmond (formerly Aligoté) was punctually awakened every day at eight (4 x 2) o'clock after eight (2 x 4) hours of refreshing sleep by one of his two private and confidential servants, South Dakota and North Dakota, dromedaries who had in the past served under him in the Dardanelles.

South Dakota, for example, would enter the Royal Bedroom with the breakfast (petit déjeuner) tray on his hump, put the tray down on the table, and announce in a bashful stentorian voice: "It is 2 x 4, Your Majesty." "Proceed, proceed," Desmond would mumble while sinking deeper into his pillow. South Dakota would then open the four windows of the Royal Bedroom, fold back the royal shutters, and immediately sunlights would come flooding into the room.

If the tale says sunlights and not sunlight, it is not, believe me, to achieve one of those "poetical" effects loathed by the tale, as it devotes itself entirely to the expression of truth, as the tale is the truth itself, and it is indeed impossible for the tale to be anything else by its very nature and essence, while poetry is untruth, be it rhymed, in which case it must unavoidably distort the truth to obey the echo, or unrhymed, which is worse, since it deceives us, in that case, about itself. The tale says "sunlights" and explains itself.

## 2  Why "sunlights"?

When the tale, not long after the Whitsun octaves and during chap. 5, section 9 of the tale (without any possible doubt one of the key moments of the tale, a turning point), had joyfully rushed—following the dog and the Princess—into Queen Botswanna's kitchen, she was in tears: "Boo boo boo boo," cried Queen Botswanna in her kitchen. And why was she crying? Because Babylas was now called Faraday, but also but maybe especially because Upholep was now her husband. But what the tale didn't relate at the time, since it was neither the time nor the place to do so, was that during that same day of the tale (the day of chap. 5, section 9), Queen Ingrid had also been crying: the reason being probably that Imogène was suddenly called Upholep, but especially that Desmond was now her husband: "Hi hi hi hi," cried Queen Ingrid in her kitchen, "what's happening to me? Hi hi hi hi."

But King Desmond, whose heart was good despite his great politeness, was grieved to find his new spouse suffering such grief in her kitchen. He called for his two private and confidential servants, the dromedaries South and North Dakota, and spoke to them more or less as follows: "Queen Ingrid, my new spouse, is suffering royal grief in her kitchen. To dispel this royal grief, which grieves me, I have decided that every morning, upon waking, the queen, through one of the windows of the Royal Bedroom, should be able to admire the sun rising in all its splendor over the hills of the kingdoms. I have spoken. So be it!"

To relate the great commotion caused in the minds of the dromedaries by these words, as the tale is now doing, can in no way mean that it can be taxed with exaggeration. To imagine that the time of Desmond's awakening, which was simply the time shown on his watch eight hours after he had gone to bed when he set it to zero o'clock, might coincide more than twice a year with the rising of the Star of the Day above the hills of the kingdoms, would be the sign of a foolish optimism. "Just get that into your hump, old chump," said South Dakota to North Dakota. "This spells destitution!" "This time it's certain, there's no way round it!" sighed North, who remembered some petty little story of date embezzlement which they had, only very recently, got away with by the skin of their yellow teeth. "What's to be done?" said North. "What's to be done?" added South.

In desperation, South Dakota picked up the telephone and dialed the number of the Sun (this number cannot be conveyed for security reasons).

### 3    "...Sol speaking. Yes?"

"Hallo," said the Sun. "Sol speaking. Yes?" (He spoke in infrared for the vowels and in ultraviolet for the consonants.)

"Hallo, South Dakota speaking, King Desmond's trusted dromedary; does Your Majesty remember me?"

"Of course I do; it was you who crossed the Libyan desert with such speed during the summer of '42, wasn't it?"

"That's me. Your Majesty has an excellent memory."

"Let's not exaggerate," said the sun jovially. "It is not every day that one sees a dromedary being chased by German tanks. And how are you?"

"Very well, thank you. And how is His Majesty yourself? and I hope your sun spots don't itch too much? fine, fine. And Her Majesty your wife? is she as well as can be? burned a little? ah ah Your Majesty always has his little joke etc... etc..." When he had thus buttonholed the Sun for a little while (if the tale dares to express itself in such a way), South Dakota decided to explain his dilemma and was happily astounded to hear himself be answered as follows:

"But of course, and with pleasure; it won't disturb me in the least, I assure you. I know how things are with queens. They are fragile beings. I, on my part, could give you many examples. There's just this one little detail, you see, I cannot have anybody being jealous — you understand, don't you? — among the nephews of King Uther Pendragon, great-uncle of Gawain, my favorite nephew. I'll have to scatter myself to the four winds, which means that you'll see four suns rising at different times over different hills. But I'm not averse to the idea of having four personalities like Pessoa. Yes, I can say that we've got a damned good idea here. Oo oo, I'm really excited. I've got a feeling it'll be a scorcher today."

## 4   One Sunday

Thus, one Sunday, at eight on the dotted dot, North Dakota, King Desmond's trusted dromedary, entered the Royal Bedroom, balancing the breakfast tray on his hump: coffee, marmalade and melted liquorice toasts for the King — tea sweetened with litchis and Turkish delight, tarama followed by moussaka for Queen Ingrid.

When Desmond had awakened the queen with a royal and conjugal tickle, the sun appeared, optimistic and glorious, over the western hills and Desmond, sipping his coffee with one hand while absentmindedly turning the financial pages of the *Kingdoms Tribune* with the other, said to North Dakota: "Fetch me my appointment book."

And the tale relates here, to be used as one sees fit, that King Desmond's appointment book showed the following time notations:

A.M.

        8:00 awak. cast. I. Breakf.
        8:30 shave
        9:00 vis. h.
        9:30 call A.
        10:00 plot in our study with U. (MYSTERY!!!!)
        12:00 Royal Lunch

P.M.

        2:00 Royal Siesta
        4:00 sail yacht with A.?

6:00-6:15 educational reading
7:00 dinner at the Princess
around 8:30 Washing up
9:00 approx. evening kiss
10:00 = 0:00 Royal beddy-byes.

## 5   Sunday 8:30 A.M. The king's Shave

When Desmond had finished his Royal Breakfast, relates the tale, he left Queen Ingrid contemplating the sun rising in all its splendor over the hills of his kingdom and retired to the kitchen to shave. His Majesty's morning shave, or Royal Shave, followed the strictest etiquette: one of the king's trusted dromedaries, North Dakota for example, started by preparing the lather in two great bowls of hot water with shaving soap scented with h.d.p.; he brought it slowly to the desired consistency by a fast retrograde and downward gyratory movement. When the lather was ready (and it could be considered ready only when it agreed, like a true aïoli sauce, to stay in the bowl when it was turned upside down), North Dakota got the straight razor out of its case and commenced the shaving operation itself, according to the immutable and traditional order following the route on the shavable surface:
a)  the chin
b)  the lower lip
c)  the right cheek
d)  the left cheek
e)  the upper lip
f)  the neck.
But careful! neither the hands of North Dakota nor his razor ever touched Desmond's royal skin at any time during the operation, as this would have constituted a crime of lèse-majesté, and possibly been punished by ablation of the hump. North Dakota, standing in front of a mirror, undertook a shaving simulacrum on the king's reflexion that was sent to him via a second mirror

*93*

by the intermediary of a third by the intermediary of a fourth in front of which Desmond, who had placed the second bowl of lather on the edge of the kitchen sink, was using his right hand to shave with a second razor, following exactly, in conformity with etiquette, the unvarying and synchronic movements of North Dakota, movements reaching him from mirror to mirror and in accordance with the Principle of Inverse Return of Light in use in the kingdoms since the time it had been promulgated by Uther Pendragon on Merlin's recommendation.

After the king's Shave, the small, even heaps of dense lather pitted with a sprinkling of royal stubble, which had been left all around a saucer, would be collected by North Dakota and placed in the museum's display cabinet.

## 6   Sunday 9:00 A.M. The harbor

Fragrant with after-shave, King Desmond left the kitchen and went to the harbor. The tale, which has already mentioned that the Princess had four uncles — Desmond, Onophriu (without an s), Upholep and Faraday — and that these uncles were kings and second cousins and had married four second cousins, would like to mention now that each king had a different job.

And the tale would like to point out, for the benefit of those who might be intrigued at the idea of kings having jobs, that this situation had been brought about by Uther Pendragon himself during the thorough economical reform he had instituted not long before dying. "It's very simple," Uther P. is reported to have said to his nephews. "Every person who is in the index will pay income tax. Kings, and queens, who are in a separate index, will pay a separate tax. Every person who doesn't figure in the separate index will be awarded a 400 percent allowance on the portion of their income tax that is not separate. Every person who pays a separate tax (except, of course, the Princess) will have to pay a 400 percent arrears increase in taxes, one month before their separate tax is due. Okay?" said Uther.

"But Uncle, how will we manage to pay income tax, separate tax and the 400 percent increase for anticipated arrears if every person liable to pay us income tax is awarded a 400 percent allowance?"

"It's very simple," answered Uther. "All you have to do is to wheel and deal. Wheel and deal, conquer markets for your kingdoms, and you'll have more than enough to pay separate tax, income tax, not forgetting the increases, the allowance, the queens' civil lists, the salaries of the alcalde, of the road man, of the Ilongot, the royalties owed to the salmon, the ducks, the sea gulls, as well as the upkeep of the Princess, the cousin's pocket money and the dog's.

"But," cried Uther's nephews once again, "how will the kingdoms — namely us — pay the exorbitant sums which the firms — again, namely us — will ask as payment for their services?"

"Nothing could be simpler," said Uther P. "With the taxes paid to you." And he died.

This is why, says the tale, the four kings had gone into business. King Desmond was a naval Architect. King Faraday was a Builder. King Onophriu (without an s) was an Editor, and King Upholep an Impostor. They wheeled huge deals, taking over huge markets and borrowing huge sums from the kingdoms which financed them by increasing the public debt to a crazy extent, paying fabulous dividends to their shareholders (the Princess, the dog, the sun, the river, Epaminondas the English squirrel, de Casimir the Canadian beaver, Solomon the salmon, Doats the four ducks, Coêors the four sea gulls, not forgetting the four anteaters and the four unicorns, the alcalde, the baker, the Ilongot, Bartleby the hedgehog, his fiancée Briolanja, and the nightingale of the Emperor of China, the twin crickets of Omsk and those of Honolulu, the four white geese, and so many others, so many others…). In short, they added every day to the general welfare. So, at nine o'clock Desmond went to the harbor, accompanied by North Dakota.

Port Desmond, at the height of development caused by the

continual expansion of the king's business, was situated on the river below the daffodil yellow lawn below the front steps, between the upstream willow and the downstream willow. It already consisted, at the time the tale is being told, of four quays, each marked off by two planks 0.40 m in length, perpendicular to the banks and hanging over the black waters where the salmon cruised. Each quay was four meters long, and the harbor could boast four docks: the Arrival dock for ships arriving; the Launching dock; the Careening dock, and the Repair dock.

The docks, at that early hour, were empty. Only around the launching dock was there any life, since the Doats, having put on their sailor's uniform, sauntered about one behind the other with an air of importance while waiting for work to start. When he saw the king, Doat 1 touched his cap with his right palm, immediately followed by Doats 2, 3, 4 respectively and successively.

"Good day, my brave lads," said Desmond. "All set?" "Yes, Your Majesty," answered Doat 1, with the warm approval of his cousins Doats 2, 3, 4 in that order and in **Anterior Duck**. Walking along the quay, Desmond reached his Company Office, a small log hut which de Casimir had built in sycamore, and crowned with a sign on which one could read GCNK (General Company for Navigation in the Kingdoms). Desmond knocked softly at the door. "Come in," said Bartleby. He went in.

## 7    Sunday 9:05 A.M.: Bartleby

The room the king had entered was small and plunged in a darkness barely pierced by the sooty glow of a candle on the desk. The exits and windows were carefully blocked and stopped up with mattresses, and the floor was heaped with innumerable sundry pieces of paper, newspapers and notebooks of all sorts, as was the desk, where they formed quite an impressive pile. Without lifting his nose from the page, Bartleby indicated to Desmond that he ought to sit down: "I'll be with you in twenty-five minutes," he said.

The registers of the General Company for Navigation in the Kingdoms were kept by Bartleby, who transcribed there, with a sea gull quill dipped in sepia and supile's ink, the movement of every ship, whether entering or leaving the harbor, as well as the names and addresses of clients, buyers or charterers.

The company's activity consisted essentially in satisfying the demands for paper boats on the parts of the children attending the schools of the kingdoms. If for example young Priscilla, caterpillar, fourth-year pupil of the junior class, Pont Vermilion school, Uncle Faraday's Road, wanted an almond green three-master to take her grandmother on a picnic to Treasure Island, she would write to Bartleby Hedgehog, Esq., c/o King Desmond, GCNK, a nice little letter in which she enclosed an order torn out of her counterfoil book, on receipt of which Bartleby would order from Marie Papers, the kingdoms' paper manufacturer, sheets of paper of the required tint, and would manufacture the boat himself in his workshop, de Casimir giving him a hand for the rudder. When the boat was finished, North Dakota would take it to the launching dock, Desmond would open a bottle of champagne, and the flimsy skiff would be launched onto the current by Doat 1, with the assistance of his three cousins, and then, abandoned to the river for a twenty-four-hour trial run, it would finally return to the arrival dock. Such was the standard procedure, which, however rational, had never functioned properly, since it so happened that, for some reason up to now never elucidated, the paper boats, once launched into the river with their crews of mayflies, never returned to where they had started, and the company had had to resign itself to sending them by post without any breaking-in, as soon as they had been christened by Desmond.

Bartleby's tasks were, it can be seen, fairly extensive. They were nevertheless not ample enough to fulfil this young genius' aspirations to glory, and Bartleby spent a great number of office hours Writing his W-Work: a bildungsroman in the great

Goethean tradition, relating the years of apprenticeship of a romantic hedgehog in London at the time of Uther Pendragon.

Yet, that morning, relates the tale, at the moment Desmond entered the room, Bartleby wasn't working on his novel, but on a poem he intended for his fiancée.

## 8  9:30 A.M.: Bartleby

Bartleby lifted his nose from his sheet of paper but, not seeing Desmond in front of him, plunged back into his poem. The tale tells us here that at this crucial moment of the tale, it is of the utmost importance that the poem Bartleby was writing be perused.

Title:
*The Poet addresses himself to his beloved and informs her, without in any way reproaching her, of the anguish occasioned, for however short a time, by her absence* [see the tale's footnote below *].

*first verse:*

Briolanja!
Oh my angel!
You are so far away that the river of my
tears is as wide as a Ganga!
And thus I play this melancholy air on my
banjo
Where is your tiny divine tongue the
colour of an aroused nymph's thigh
Where are the $10^{14}$ heavenly quills and
your four tender thigh-
bones.

---

*(Tale's footnote: Bartleby's poems have been published by Faraday, on behalf and to the great pleasure of the New Kingdoms Press.)

Such was the first verse, with its two magnificent rhymes in
**inthigh**
But when he attacked the second verse, which he wanted, following there the old tradition of the troubadour hedgehogs, to be exactly *unisonante*, that is to say, with the same rhymes, Bartleby found himself confronted with an unexpected difficulty. The first line would, of course, be
**Briolanja!**
But, having already used "angel" in the first verse, he was momentarily short of bisyllabic words in "-anja" whose density and nobility would match his conception. And this is why he would have liked Desmond's advice.

But, says the tale, Desmond, according to the schedule noted in his diary, had, at 9:30 on the dot, gone to the telephone box situated to the right of Bartleby's office and partitioned off by a thin wall of cigarette papers of the Job brand; it so happened that Bartleby, like all hedgehogs, was quite obviously absentminded, and that his absentmindedness was compounded by the superhuman effort required to hunt out this reluctant rhyme in "anja," indispensable for the second line of the second verse of his poem, transcribed on his paper without realizing it was the last sentence pronounced by Desmond during his telephone conversation. A gesture, says the tale, pregnant with incalculable consequences.

The paper bore the following:

*second verse:*

**Briolanja!**
**I cannot find any rhyme for "anja"; I must**
**find a rhyme for "anja".**
**Let's meet at four o'clock on the yacht? Okay?**

When he had written these last words, Bartleby, more and more absentminded, folded the sheet in four and placed it, as if the poem was finished, in an envelope addressed to his fiancée, which he then put on top of the Special Delivery pile.

## 9 At four o'clock in the afternoon, on King Desmond's yacht

The yacht yawed sluggishly in the breeze. The sun, re-unified, shone with kindness on the gleaming surface of the clear water where the salmon was cruising for his afternoon meditation. Through the Portholes, the Bulwarks and the Hatchways, as well as through the Fo'c'sle [*false indication* — **tale's note**], poured out floods of ancient music:

*"There are no flies on Auntie, on Auntie, on Auntie,*
*There are no flies on Auntie*
*And I will tell you why*

*She's not what you'd call hideous*
*But the flies are so fastidious..."*

Let's follow the song, if you don't mind, back to the source of the sound and let's throw an indiscreet glance into the cabin, where the gramophone is shouting itself hoarse with the refrain

*"Oh there are no flies on Auntie, on Auntie..."*

There are three people in the cabin, not counting the already mentioned gramophone and a cinematograph screen: the first is King Desmond, the second is Queen Adirondac (can you believe it? Queen Adirondac is at this moment in the cabin of King Desmond's yacht. Could it be that she, then, is the mysterious A., who is mentioned twice in the king's appointment book?)

And what about the third? — the third is a young woman whom we still don't know. Her name is Brigid, but such a Scandinavianesque-sounding name should not conceal the fact that she is actually a young pink California crane. The

100

gramophone is pouring out floods of music, King Desmond and Queen Adirondac are stretched on deck chairs, patented as being non-overturnable and unsinkable, and what are they doing?

We glue our eye to the porthole, the better to see what King Desmond, Queen Adirondac and young Brigid, the pink California crane, are doing, at four o'clock in the afternoon, on three deck chairs, in the cabin of King Desmond's yacht. So, what *are* they doing?

They are eating a giant strawberry sundae drenched in melted marshmallow with boysenberry syrup, crowned with a high peak of pink whipped cream from "Chantilly, Pennsylvania," and studded with frozen raspberries. Desmond is attacking it from the top with his wooden spoon, Brigid and Adirondac, each on her own side with their fingers! Their faces are distorted by greediness; the spoon and fingers never stop penetrating ever further inside the creamy mass of the sundae, while the boysenberry syrup and the melted marshmallow run down their wrists, down their cheeks and into their eyes! Their eyes are glued to the screen and on this screen a strangely similar scene is taking place: another immense strawberry sundae, absolutely similar to the first one, is giving way before an attack by the spoon and fingers of some characters caught by the camera. Who can these people be? We get as close as possible and we recognize ... ****, the famous oil tycoon, the beautiful Ava G.; and the third (for there are three characters on the screen, as there are three in the cabin), the third is that young slim pink child, as pink as the pink ice cream, as pink as whipped cream from Chantilly, Pennsylvania? Yes, you've guessed right: none other than Brigid, who has come straight from California with her film, in which, by the way, if one were to look closely at the background (the scene shown is the cabin of a yacht anchored in a Sunset Boulevard swimming pool), one could see another screen in which the pink Brigid is licking another giant strawberry sundae in the company of the Pr... of U... and the Q... of En... what? no? ... do excuse the tale, but strong pressure is being applied to it not to divulge these names, for security reasons.

The last notes of "There Are No Flies on Auntie" die inside the wax of the record, the last pink spoonfuls of ice cream disappear between sated lips. With a sad movement of the head, we remove our eye from the porthole before it remains glued to it and we leave behind us, far away, King Desmond's yacht.

How innocent nature appears: the sun shines; the river runs, trembling with light. The salmon meditates.

## 10   8:00 P.M.: Dining room in the Princess's castle

The scene represents the Princess's dining room in the Princess's castle. Around the table can be seen in this order: the Princess; King Desmond; Queen Ingrid; King Faraday; Queen Eleonore; the dog; King Onophriu; Queen Adirondac; King Upholep; Queen Botswanna; the Princess; King Desmond; Queen Ingrid; King Faraday; Queen Eleonore; the dog; King Onophriu; Queen Adirondac; King Upholep; Queen Botswanna; the Princess; King Desmond; Queen Ingrid; King Faraday; Queen Eleonore; the dog; King Onophriu; etc....

A glass of Apfelsaft stands on a pedestal table. In the left-hand corner of the stage, facing the audience, an object cast in plaster representing a Bass clef flanked by two quavers. To the right, an Epigone, immobile; Chalky wig; golden Buttons; Poulaine shoes; Martingales. Through the half-drawn curtains one or two bits of landscape can be seen: Marihuana Bushes; Chinese Cabbage. A Lemur and a Lion go up and down a slide. An Iroquois chief goes by on his Toboggan. [*This passage is simply full of false indications, as well as false false indications* — the tale]

KING DESMOND [*ostensibly, to Queen Ingrid*]: A second helping of this excellent gooseberry boutifara, dear?

[*A majordomo rushes in*]

A MAJORDOMO: Princess, a call for you on the telephone.

THE PRINCESS [*addressing herself to the queens, the kings, the dog*]: Excuse me a second. [*She goes out.*]

QUEEN BOTSWANNA [*with a restlessness she does not manage to hide from the audience*]: Who can it be? at this time?

KING FARADAY [*with forced joviality*]: It might be an inspector from Scotland Yard

Ha ha ha ha [*nobody laughs*]

[*8:01 P.M.: the Princess's telephone*]

THE PRINCESS: Hallo

BARTLEBY'S VOICE: Hallo, who do you want to speak to?

THE PRINCESS: Is that you, Bartleby?

BARTLEBY'S VOICE [*surprised*]: Yes, it's me.

THE PRINCESS: Get a grip. Remember, it was **you** who called **me.**

BARTLEBY'S VOICE: That's true. Where's my head? Princess, Princess, something horrible has happened. Briolanja has vanished!

THE PRINCESS: Are you sure you didn't go to the wrong house?

BARTLEBY'S VOICE: I am, I assure you. In any case, I've got my glasses on.

THE PRINCESS: I'm coming.

# Chapter 9

## The Dog's Afternoon

### 1 It was raining

It was raining. It had been raining continuously on the kingdoms
for four days. In Queen Adirondac's kitchen a lovely fire of Judas-tree wood was blazing. In Queen Eleonore's kitchen a
lovely fire of Gum-tree wood was blazing. A lovely fire of El-
der-tree wood was blazing in Queen Botswanna's kitchen and in
Queen Ingrid's kitchen a lovely fire of Almond-tree wood. Thus,
says the tale, a warm glow prevailed in the queens' kitchens.

It was raining. It had been raining continuously on the kingdoms for four days.

In Queen Adirondac's kitchen, where a lovely fire of Judas-
tree wood was blazing, the queen and the Princess were sitting in
front of a large bowl of jujube Bovril. At the Princess's feet was
the dog lying. A lovely fire of Judas-tree was burning. It was
raining.

And Queen Adirondac, holding the steaming bowl of jujube
Bovril in her hands to warm them, to the Princess was saying:
"You see, it's not so much the fact that King Onophriu (without
an s) is now suddenly called Avogadr (without an o) that bothers
me, it's not so much that Desmond is called Gustave, nor that
Jugurtha is now my husband that bothers me. It's that I don't
love him!" "Who?" said the Princess. "Who what?" said the
queen. "Who is it you don't love?" "But, Faraday, of course, my
husband, I mean Jugurtha. That's his name all of a sudden. But
I'm now in love with Upholep, I mean Eponyme (that's his name
all of a sudden). I've got Eponyme under my skin. You see,

that's what's bothering me. That's why I'm asking for your advice."

"How come?" said the Princess. "You're now in love with Imogène? I mean Upholep at this time? I mean Eponyme all of a sudden? And what is Botswanna going to say?" "Botswanna?" said the queen. "Do you really think Botswanna cares? Eponyme is her husband, but it's not him she's in love with. You see, she's in love with Jugurtha all of a sudden." "And what about Ingrid?" said the Princess. "She's in love with Gustave." "Gustave!" said the Princess. "Has she told you that?" "No," said the queen, "but I'm sure of it." "How?" said the Princess. "It's really terribly simple," said Adirondac. "She looks deep into Babylas's eyes. I mean Faraday's. I mean Jugurtha's. And she tells him. What a beautiful job you're doing, how exalting it must be to be a builder, to constantly be building buildings, and bo on and bo borth... and as it is Avogadr (without an o) who is her husband, I'm quite sure that means that it is Desmond. I mean Gustave. With whom she's in love." "Ah...," said the Princess, "all this is **very** interesting, but tell me. Where..."

At that moment Queen Adirondac put her steaming bowl of jujube Bovril down on the table and, bringing one finger to her lips, said "sh" while looking at the dog who was lying at the feet of the Princess. And the Princess looked at the dog who was lying at the feet of the Princess. Then the Princess and the queen looked at the dog and the Princess said: "Dog, would you be kind enough to please go and see whether I happen to be on the lawn? And do not forget your galoshes and your umbrella. It's raining."

## 2   The dog goes out on the front steps

When the dog, with his four galoshes around his neck and his open umbrella in his left fore-paw, came out on the front steps, the rain had just stopped, to be replaced by a shower pounding away on the slates of Jugurtha's roof, giving a copious wetting to the King's jockeys, who were dressed up as Numidian horsemen behind the chimneys. "This won't do their numidity any good!" said the dog to himself with a bitter grin, for he hated being sent down to the sopping wet lawn to go and see whether the Princess was there (when he knew perfectly well that she wasn't), and this at the precise moment when highly interesting revelations, which would have greatly enhanced his knowledge of life, were about to go back and forth across the kitchen table. Being now slightly more serene after his thought about the jockeys, the spice of which he promised to share with his friends Epaminondas (the English squirrel) and Solomon (the salmon), he took a few steps on the lawn. But he was hampered by his umbrella. So he entrusted it to the river, which had got out of its bed to escape the shower and was now lounging in the middle of the grass, begging it to bring the thing back to him in four hours. He stood a little while on the front steps, not knowing what to do, in the unending rain. He thought of his bones which would be drenched, but he didn't have the courage to dig them up and put them under cover in the boat garage. He yawned two or three times while scratching his occiput and farted once or twice. Then, says the tale, he decided to go for a walk.

## 3    In the forest

In the forest the shower made a confidential rustling while chattering onto the leaves of the tall age-old trees before falling on the ground among the *club moss*, the **mushrooms** and the **lichen**, with a soft gentle hiss [*this is a false indication*]. The dog, his four galoshes bouncing about around his neck, walked up an oblique path. Lined with dark and huge cypresses, with insane pine trees, with enormous oak trees. The sky was entirely cast with the thick, shadowy clouds of the shower, the trees opposed the entire force of their leaves to the penetration of daylight, and the dog was becoming very frightened; he could hear his galoshes bouncing and knocking together around his neck, and for a little while now this noise had become louder and stranger; and he suddenly realized that the din the galoshes made was now compounded with the noise of his teeth chattering at a rate of 89 clicks a minute. He thought of turning round, of going back. Too late. His paws moved him up the alley despite his will. Moved by *la forza del destino*, prey to an incompressible terror, the dog went on. And found himself in a clearing. And in this dark clearing (the last straw for a clearing) he vaguely noticed a number of alleys branching out. The alleys coming out of the clearing, says the tale, were six in number. At the beginning of the first alley was written "first alley"; at the beginning of the second was written "second alley"; and so forth; but, says the tale, the dog was prey to such a panic that, without bothering to think for a second about the possible destination of these alleys, though these had been indicated by the tale, he dived nose first into alley number one.

## 4    The child in the tree

The alley was like a dark tunnel that had been dug into the dark canopy of trees, but right at the end something like a small glow could be made out. Toward this glow the dog rushed. With desperate energy. Gradually the glow became a vast brightness and this brightness was that of a tree, very straight and weighed down with bright candelles glowing like starres; this is how the tale puts it. And right on top of the trees sat a completely naked child who brighter and more radiant than the candelles seemeth. And the child looked at the dog with a smile but did not say anything. *"Child, child,"* shouted the dog, *"can you tell me what this tale hides from me?"* "How could I tell you," said the child, "I'm too young. But in any case, my poor dog, you haven't reached the end of your troubles. You're not in the correct tale, you see. This is the first tale, and it isn't meant for dogs." Having spoken, the child started climbing up faster and faster from branch to branch and when he reached the very top the candelles went out and the tree vanished. The dog found himself right back in the clearing and entered the second alley.

## 5  The retinue

He barely had time to take a few steps when a castle came toward him. It was large and imposing and stood by deep and steepe waters. Just as the dog was putting his paw to the door it opened and servants rushed out with a large, hot and deliciously scented bath towel. When they had perfectly rubbed the dog inside and out so as to properly dry his fur, they took him to a vast room where a king sat.

THE KING: Friend, you will not mind, I hope, if I do not rise to welcome you properly, but I am not very free in my movements.

THE DOG: *Do not worry in the least, I assure you that I am perfectly all right as I am.*

THE KING: Come to me and fear not. Sit down here on the bed, next to me. Where are you coming from today?

THE DOG: *I left the Princess's castle not very long ago. It was raining.*

THE KING: God be with you, but that is a jolly long trot.

There is more light in the room, says the tale, than could be produced by all the candles in a castle. A young man comes out of a room with a white lance which he grips round the middle. He passes between the fire and the bed where the king and the dog have sat to chat. The lance is white, as is its tip. A drop of blood has formed at the end of the sharp tip and this drop falls to touch the hand of the man holding the lance. The dog sees this marvel and is surprised. The young man bears a strong resemblance to the astronomer and the dog would very much like to ask the king the reason for all this but he daren't as he recalls what the Princess has told and taught him, that too much talking is harmful. He is afraid, if he were to ask a question, of being thought too canine. At that moment a damsel enters the room carrying a large dish. On this large dish has been placed a bone, of such succulence that the dog's mouth starts watering. The damsel is so beautiful that she is almost as beautiful as the Princess and when she moves toward the dog she gives out a soft light of such mellowness that the candles lose their sparkle as the stars do whenever the Princess's eyes turn toward the dog. The young woman crosses the room and disappears quickly into another room. The dog watches her go past and would very much like to ask to whom this bone is going to be given, but he daren't. Could it be that he has remained silent for too long? At times too much silence is not much better than too much talking. As the Princess is later to say to the dog, "It was a fantastic opportunity to clear some of the tales' mysteries, and you threw it away." At any rate, he stays silent, the king and the castle vanish, and he find himself once again in the clearing with his galoshes round his neck, at the entrance of the third alley.

## 6   Lagado

In the third alley, says the tale, the dog came across a "party" of Lagadonians who were on their way to the Court for an afternoon of conversation.

It has been quite a while, as everyone knows, since the Lagadonians, those postmodern linguists, philosophically as well as pragmatically corrected the defects of languages, imperfect in that words, as you surely know, can be given various meanings. How perverse, they say, to confer to *day* and to *night*, contradictorily, here a dark tone, there a bright one. As thinking is like speaking or writing, but without props, so the diversity, on Earth, of idioms, prevents us from uttering words which would otherwise express by themselves, through a unique temper of the blacksmith, God, materially like the tale, Truth. In short, since words are only names for things, the Lagadonians have understood that it would be more convenient, practical and efficient for men to carry upon their backs such things as were necessary to express the ideas or thoughts they might want to discourse about with their fellow men. If they want to talk about Burdock, they take Burdock with them; if they want to talk about Analysis situs, they take with them a treatise in topology as well as a few atlases; if Ideology appeals to them they take six tea chests full of it. And, if Electrons, they nab half a dozen in a box. Nothing easier.

And this, says the tale, was how, on this showery afternoon, the Lagadonians were proceeding while going to Court for a meeting with their king, followed by their servants, who were pulling a cart full of the commodities of conversation. When they espied the dog, they politely stopped, and one of them took out of his pocket a huge question mark, showed it to the dog and waited. When the dog expressed his desire to be given, if at all possible, some indication that might prove helpful in deciphering the tale and the mysteries accumulating therein, they smiled with a whiff of commiseration at his slightly archaic means of communicating, but, as they were of a polite nature, they let it pass; and the most venerable among them, no doubt a distinguished scientist if one were to judge from the immense quantity of vocabulary in his possession, and which completely filled no less than four converted first-class carriages of the Trans-Kingdom Express Company, took out from the third carriage an immense folio volume, which he placed silently before the paws of the dog. Who opened the book and read, on the title page: ——
———, Third Tale of Labrador [the title of the "third Tale of Labrador" is left out by the tale, as a precaution]. *"I thank you,"* said the dog, *"but this isn't the one I'm looking for."* And with a deep bow, he went on.

## 7    The encounter with the snail

It was raining unremittingly in the clearing where the dog, after three unsuccessful attempts at the alleys, found himself stuck yet again with his soggy galoshes, his anxiety and his wet fur.

The obscurity was still inquietous ["inquietous": of disturbing, menacing, fateful aspect; *caninism* — **tale's note**] and difficult to penetrate, and it even looked as if it had a certain tendency to thicken, which seemed to be a sign that the afternoon, wearing on, despite the shower, would not be long in changing into evening. The dog was seized by a feeling of urgency and he hastened to enter another alley.

It was a path invaded by grass and flanked by a small dry-stone wall (which was in fact sopping wet) crowned with Olive trees, Almond trees, Vines, and Thyme; which showed without any doubt that one was on a Provençal path and in the country which, as everyone knows, adjoins the kingdoms on the eastern side. The path was just about to vanish in the scrubland-like moors when the dog noticed in front of him a huge fennel plant, on whose highest tuft was a snail, its horns quivering toward the sky. The soft damp flesh of the snail hugged the stem of the fennel and at the same time held a six-stringed viola da gamba, on which he played suavissimo in "oda continua" (continuous melody) while singing in a consonantal voice a poem whose shape had great beauty and sophistication and which the dog, who had no idea what it was all about, except for the few words "quan la seror de mon oncle," did not fail to admire. After he had discreetly waited for the six verses and the envoi of the song to finish, the dog dared to cough lightly to attract the snail's attention. Forthwith the snail lowered dreamily toward the dog its two great peduncled eyes and said to him: "How pleasing is a demand such as yours / I am Arnaut Danieldzoï, and I weep and go singing / Eyes turned toward the spiral nebulae / I still believe my song can reach. / I pray you, valorous dog / When you have delivered the Princess / Remember in time my terrible pain." At that moment, the wind coming from the forest bent the fennel down to the grass, where the snail slid and vanished, leaving behind a ribbon of silver slime.

## 8    Meeting between the dog and the Founder-President

The dog now found himself on a wide majestic avenue lined with elms, beeches and birches. The street sign was hanging halfway up a lamppost, and the dog, pushing the hair out of his eyes and hoisting himself up on his back legs, managed to read:

### Queen Tharama's Road

Along the avenue stood a prim little cottage, the door of which possessed an ancient door-knocker, underneath which could be read:

Efellel, Fresident-Pounder of Oulipo.
Enter without knocking or knock without entering
(as you wish)

The dog scratched the lower part of the door and it opened. After going through an entrance hall and pushing open a second door, he found himself in a small sunny garden, bathed in roses and raspberries. At his table, under the protection of an arbor, with his dressing gown on, sat the President-Founder of Oulipo.

"Do sit down, my friend, I was expecting you. I don't think Raymond will be long in coming."

The dog sat down. On the table, in front of the President, was a huge alephourteen-dimensional chessboard of which the dog could only make out, darkly, a few details. From time to time the President, whose eyes shone from behind his round spectacles, would move his hand toward one of the pieces, then hesitate, take it back, inwardly relishing some improbable strategy, grasp the piece, put it down, and once more remove it. Although the circumstances made him nervous, the dog was not long in noticing when he looked closer that inside the chess pieces dwelt a multitude of tiny little fellows, very busy, armed with paper, pencils, compasses, fountain pens, calculators, restless with an intense intellectual frenzy which pushed them, with incredible speed, to write, cross out, compose, dispose, express, impress, depress, draw, play, demonstrate, deduct, hunt out, understand, withstand, stand trial, and many other things.

Efellel glanced briefly toward the end of the garden, behind the arbor, as if he had heard steps; his hand came to rest on a golden bell, on the table, to his left: "Would you like, dog, to partake of a light meal with us? Marie-Adèle has cooked a very good haricot mutton." *"No, no,"* said the dog, *"don't trouble yourself; I assure you I cannot stay much longer; the Princess is expecting me for tea."* "That's a shame," said Efellel dreamily, while glancing again over his shoulder. "I don't think Raymond will be much longer now." And noticing how the dog looked with fascination at the pieces of the game spread in front of him, he added: "This, you see, is the workshop of my ⊙∪-×-℘⊙. These little fellows you see here are my assistants the Oulilliputians. In bygone days, when I... when we, Raymond and I, created the Oulipo, I gathered around us a few young men, mathematicians and poets, the Oulipians, to whom I would give my precious directives for the carrying-out of the most urgent tasks of Potentiality. But work, you see, wasn't making much progress. They were certainly very willing, but so slow! so timorous! They wouldn't accept that one Ouvroir wasn't sufficient for the task, that Potentiality is infinite, transfinite even. There is so much to do, so much to do! But I don't want to bore you with all that. You have come to ask me for advice, it seems."

*"I would like,"* said the dog timidly, *"I would like you, if you have a minute to spare, to give me an indication."*

"Which tale are you in, exactly?"

*"In the fourth,"* said the dog. "The Princess Hoppy, or the Fourth Tale of Labrador." The President got out of his desk drawer a big book, and browsed through it while saying absentmindedly: "Four, four, a very beautiful number; very remarkable, remarkable! not as beautiful as Euler's Constant, certainly, but remarkable, remarkable... Ah, here we are." He bent

down towards the book, took off his spectacles, wiped them clean, looked again, and said: "I'm terribly sorry, but I don't seem to be able to read what my secretary has written; her writing is getting worse and worse; I'll have to do something about it; but no, really, I can't tell you anything."

And yet the dog, even at a distance, from across the table, which was very big, had the strong impression that the writing was perfectly legible, and clear, and that the President was not telling him the complete truth. But could he do anything about it? He got up to take his leave.

"You're not going already, are you?" said Efellel. "Won't you wait for Raymond? Never mind, never mind; but take this with you, it's only something to read; it's an offprint of my last Manifesto, the *Transfinite Manifesto of Potentiality*. And from behind his spectacles, he threw the dog a kind glance. The dog thanked him profusely and went away.

As he was leaving, he heard the President say, to someone who was arriving and whom he did not see: "Poor little one, yes poor little one."

In the avenue, under the light of a lamppost, the dog tried to glance at the *Manifesto*. Unfortunately, all the first pages were blank, those which had been numbered, 1, 2, 3, 4, and so on following the well-ordered sequence of natural numbers, including the page omega plus one, which meant that the dog would have had to browse through an infinity of pages before really starting his reading; and he was not certain of being able to achieve this in a finite time. In any case not before tea time. So he regretfully abandoned the task.

## 9   The menace

Queen Tharama's Road, says the tale, adjoins the kingdoms at their southern border, which it crosses by means of a bridge suspended above a fearsome torrent.

It was raining. The shower had retreated at the approach of

night, and had again given way to pouring rain. And the dog was hurrying along in the rain, puzzled, tired, wet through to the roots of his fur. His galoshes, full of the liquid whose density is 1, weighed heavy around his neck.

As he was about to step onto the suspended bridge, he noticed a silhouette in front of him; and this silhouette was not that of an innocuite [*caninism* — **the tale**] and transhumant traveler such as one sometimes encounters at the crossings of bridges suspended above the torrents of our terraqueous globe. It was the solid and dark silhouette of a threatening, frightful gallows bird.

Threatening and frightful to the dog's eyes was the look of the creature that stood in front of him on the suspended bridge and barred his way. He seemed to be some nameless mixture of Turk, Privateer and Semanticist. He wore baggy trousers; in one hand he held a saber and in the other a blunderbuss; on his head he wore a hat as black as a soul dipped in ink and over one eye a bandage, also black. And, what was probably the worst, he had a wooden leg; it was a woody wooden leg (the left one, the most sinister) made in equal parts of four varieties: Acacia, Ipecacuanha, Birch, and Pond Elm; and while darting the sparkling and malevolent glance of his single eye at the dog, with his wooden leg he beat on the ground the first four bars of the "Turkish March," which was causing the bridge to begin vibrating dangerously.

## "DOG,"

screamed the foul apparition with such a loud voice that the tale has been forced to indicate it by using a capital outline font set in 18 points,

## "DOG,
## AT LONG LAST WE MEET.

# COME HERE AND FIGHT WITH ME,
# IF YOU'RE A MAN!"

*"But I'm not a man,"* mumbled the dog, his teeth chattering. *"I'm a dog."*

# "COME AND FIGHT NEVERTHELESS, WRETCHED AND CANINE DOG, ONE OF US SHOULD NOT BE ON THIS EARTH; AND THAT ONE IS YOU."

Hearing this, the dog did not hesitate for more than a second. Taking to his paws (which was quite a business as he had his galoshes around his neck) he got off the bridge at a speed of 317 meters per second and threw himself into the torrent. The torrent immediately engulfed him in its uproar, but he was able to hear, before going under, these terrible words:

# "BEWARE! TAKE GOOD CARE OF THE PRINCESS!"

At last the bank was near. Helped by the ducks, he climbed onto the grass, and staggered on, shaking with cold, rain and terror, towards the front steps. The river had waited a long time to give him back his umbrella but, having other business on hand and not wanting to risk inundating King Jugurtha's territory, it had gone, taking along a bit of lawn for its five o'clock tea.

"Well, where have you been? what took you so long?" began the Princess, but she immediately stopped. The dog was out of sorts, soaking wet, frissoning; there was madness in his eyes, he shivered, he laughed, he was delirious. "He's ill!" shouted the Princess and the queen. The dog felt himself being wrapped up in a bathrobe and placed on a stretcher, to be taken, probably, to his kennel."No! no!" cried he. "Not her! not her!"

Before sinking and losing consciousness, he saw above him the gray-blue eyes of the Princess, worried and soft, and he felt a kiss on the fever-hot fur of his cheeks.

**coda   The tale takes its leave**

It was a beautiful temporarily final July morning of the tale (and in any case, says the tale, like every morning, finally, temporary) and the dog was cured of his fever and of his terror thanks to Antibiotics, to Venetian Balms, to Inguents, to Embrocations and especially, especially, to the Princess's kisses, was taking a walk by the river with Bartleby and Epaminondas, and the lawn was red with joy and poppies. Bartleby and the English squirrel asked him how far he had gone with his investigation.

*"I know everything,"* said the dog modestly. *"Or more exactly I know everything that can be known in the present state of the tale. I know everything that can be known, everything that cannot now be known, everything that can be guessed without one really being sure of knowing it, everything else that should be known if one wanted to know everything. I have published a small brochure at the New Kingdom Press, where I have written down a bit of every-*

*thing, under the form of*

            *Questions for Listeners to the Tale.*

*"The tale,"* said the dog, *"will place these in the Appendix to the first part of the Fourth Tale of Labrador. Look, I have prepared a copy for each of you of the manuscript and with a dedication."*

It was the peaceful hour, the hour when the lions have not yet come to drink, and the tale was getting ready to take its leave.

"Yes," said Bartleby, "that's all very well and good, but who has kidnapped my fiancée?" *"I don't know,"* said the dog, *"I don't know yet; I have a little idea. But, be assured that we will do our utmost, the Princess and I, to find her; as well as the cousins."*

And with these words of hope, says the tale, the tale took its leave.

# Appendix

## 79 Questions for Listeners to the Tale
### by The Dog

*seasoned with Complementary Advice and served with the Index and the Separate Index.*

### Preface

*I have no idea of my origins. As far back as I can remember, I have always been at the service of the Princess and, in my memory, no canine paternal nose, no warm, sloppy maternal tongue comes and leans over my cradle. I sometimes fancy that I come of royal, or at least princely, ancestry, and I question the Princess about my childhood; she smiles, looks at me with her incomparable, beautiful gray-blue eyes, and changes the subject.*

*From a very tender age, I was enraptured by numbers, in all their manifestations; not only the modern number, the abstract number, the arithmetical number, the rational, real, complex, quaternionic, Cayleian, non-standard, supernatural, rhythmic, Peanian, Russelian, Geralducian, Conwayian, Badiouesque, Fregean, Benabian, Lussonian, Quenellian, Nelsonian, cardinal, ordinal, finite or transfinite number; but also, and even more so, the one that, pregnant with concrete figures, enumerates, notes, shows, orders, evokes, combines, permutes, unfolds dancing stars in front of my eyes, unfolds shadows, barks, as well as bones, raspberry charlottes and kisses. A poetics of numbers exists, which I would like one day to come back to.*

*What a tremendous fate is that of number: integer or fractional, imaginary or real, it always carries with it the divine utopian character. It ceaselessly, almost, contradicts the oblivion of not being anymore. In prison, through a succession of lines written in blood on the walls, it becomes patience, and revolt. At the hospital window, it is the glowing hope of getting better. It is everywhere the negation of disorder, of confusion, of iniquity. At night, on my poor opossum-hair palliasse, tortured by the anguish of absence and deprivation, under the constant threat of the four Interior and Exterior Dangers, I count. And counting the telltale number is my consolation.*

*In this opuscule, I have put together a few questions that naturally come to mind at this point in the tale, and which listeners to this tale are bound to have asked themselves while listening to it. To these questions, no answers will be given. Listeners to the tale, after having carefully listened to the tale, are perfectly able to find them by themselves. They will constitute, in short, Exercises, which will enable them to check whether they have properly taken in the tale. The most difficult are marked \*, \*\*, \*\*\*, even \*\*\*\* if necessary.*

**Questions about the Tale Dedication** (see p. 127)

1    "Adventure, Algebra, Blonde, Barbary, Blank, Elegant, Insensible, Irreducible, Enigma": justify the use of these words.

2    "In this our century...": Where does this passage come from?

3    "Ah Princess...": Find the line of poetry that is used here by the Tail as a model.

## Questions about Chapter 0

4      § 10: At a rough guess, how many?

5****    § 31: Translate into English the **last indication**.

*Comment: Snigger on my part. Everyone pretends that Dog is a gross language, infinitely less complex, efficient and subtle than Greek, Poldevian or Nial. Be that as it may: no one, and I repeat no one, has so far been able to translate the last Indication about what the tale says, yet it is luminous and quasi transparent. Now, it is of course composed in superior Dog and not in ordinary Dog; nevertheless!*

## Questions about Chapter 1

6      Could you make some suggestions as to possible locations for the kingdoms of Eleonor (without an e) and Imogène?

Note: For reasons of security, answers to question 6 should be sent encoded in **superior Dog**, in a sealed envelope addressed to "Dog, Esq., The Princess's Castle, The Kingdoms."

7*    § 7: Give an algebraic interpretation of the Rule of Saint Benedict.

Footnote: During a reading of the tale by the dog in front of the SEMTA (State Education Mathematics Teachers Association) not one listener to the tale was able to answer this question in less than three minutes.

8      § 8: Translate from **ordinary Dog** the answer of the dog to the Princess.

9      Deduce from the preceding the reason why the dog answers "Yes" to the Princess.

10    § 9: Why do the queens pot while the kings plot?

## About Chapter 2

11*    § 1: What effect do the hazelnuts have on the salmon?

12**    § 2: Explain the links between the game of G W D D B W L L and rugby.

13    § 3: How many different layouts are available to the dog when he lays out his bone collection? (It is important to make a careful distinction between the two meanings of "lay out" in the wording of this question.)

14    Justify the choice of bone varieties buried by the dog.

15    Translate what the dog says to the Princess.

§ 4: The events of the Princess's family history related at this number belong to the "First Tale of Labrador."

About which one would be advised to consult, for example (and with all necessary reservations), the elementary (and not devoid of inaccuracies) work by Jacques Roubaud entitled *Graal-Fiction*.

16    Why is the cypress from Iceland, the hazelnut barometer and the coconut eglantine?

17    § 6 & 8: Formulate and answer a pertinent question about the bilberries.

18    § 6: Fill in the three dots after "ref" in the sentence pronounced by Imogène.

19    § 7: **Anthracite** is an ancient variety of coal (carbon) which, in the old days, was burned in stoves for heating. In the kingdoms, like everywhere else, anthracite ovoids were oval, but in the kingdoms they had the property of being, on an horizontal projection, Cassini's ovals. Write the equation, in Cartesian coordinates, the inch being the unit of length, of an anthracite ovoid weighing 4 x 4 ounces.

20      § 8: Describe the process used by the dog to cross the river.

21      § 10: After "black glove" a segment of sentence has unfortunately been left out (these are the hazards of oral transmission); restore with the use of chapter 6.

## About Chapter 3

22      § 1: Indicate the source of the first sentence of the story of the young man from Baghdad.

23      § 2: "in the arms of the Indus..." Why does the dog say "Oh!" at that moment?

24      Recite the multiplication table modulo eighteen.

25      § 3: Why is the astronomer examining the "sixth sector of the sky"?

26***   § 6: It is high time for the listener to show some imagination. Can you formulate a hypothesis as to why the astronomer did not find in his notebook the coordinates of the window glanced at at dawn on the fourth of June?

27*     § 8: Justify the presence in the light spectrum of the four rays mentioned, emitted by the eyes of the astronomer's beloved.

28      § 9: Indicate the three sources for the first paragraph in that section.

29**    § 10: Find one or two of these "two or three details" which had struck the Princess while eluding the dog *(who, if you are able to answer that question, would be very happy to be informed of it)*.

## About Chapter 4

30*     § 6: How do we know that it is Eleonor's turn, that evening, to give the royal kiss?

31      § 8: What does the dog say?

32** Compare the various examples of **"ordinary Dog"**
so far given by the tale, and deduce from them how
that language is articulated.

33*** "Et la quatrième?" Yes indeed, and the fourth?

34 § 9: What does the dog say when he says **"ut"**?

35 Why does the dog say what he says when he says **"ut"**?

36 How does the robot begotten by the astronomer
function?

## About Chapter 00

37 Solve question a.

38 Answer question g.

39* Comment on the clue.

40** Comment on the other clue.

41**** Decipher the new last indication.

## About Chapter 5

42** Why is Eleonor now called Onophriu (without an s)?

43** Why "now"?

44* Find likely kingdoms for Desmond and Faraday.

45 Find the difference between "security" and "precaution."

46 Why are the dog and the Princess now playing croquet?

47 Translate what the dog says in § 4.

48* Compare the **ordinary Dog** language in chap. 5 to
that in the one before.

49 Compare (§ 6) the Rule of Saint Benedict with the
Rule of Saint Origen.

50 Who is the poet reporting the advice to the dog in
§ 8?

51**** Decipher the new indication in **confidential Dog** in
§ 8.

Note: the peculiarities of grasshopper language will be specified in later chapters.

52       What does the dog say in § 9?

## About Chapter 6

53       Make some pertinent stylistic comments about § 1.

54       Justify Ermengarde's reading (§ 2).

**Careful! Do not attempt to find out who the Stone Guest is.**

55a     Translate the tale into **Posterior Duck**.

55b     Translate the tale into **Anterior Duck**.

56       Translate the tale translated into **Posterior Duck** into **Reverse Anterior Duck**.

57       What does Doat 1 say (§ 6)?

58       Complete the dog's answer to question a of the booby-trap exercise.

59       Complete the dog's answer to question b of the booby-trap exercise.

60       Complete the dog's answer to question c of the booby-trap exercise.

61*      What does the dog answer to question d of the booby-trap exercise.

62       Solve the ABC.

63**    Answer the *extra-credit question* of the ABC.

64       What is the mistake found by the Princess in the second verse of the four operations incantation?

65*      The same verse contains, in fact, a second mistake. Which one?

66       Suggest some versions of the third and fourth verses of the incantation.

## About Chapter 7

67**    Why does the tale say, in a curious manner, "he was in his element, de Casimir was"?

68    Do you notice anything particular about the astronomer's superior in rank (§ 2)?

69    Explain the other eight Christian names of Marie-Josèphe, before and after the fourth of August.

70    Justify the dog's preoccupations in § 10.

71*   Why are the king's jockeys hidden among the slates of the roof?


## About Chapter 8

72    Taking into account the rest of the chapter, clarify the entries in Desmond's appointment book.

73**  Put forward some serious hypotheses that might explain the non return of the paper boats to their original dock (§ 7).

74    Suggest four rhymes for "anja" for verses 2 to 6 of Bartleby's poem.

75    Find some false indications and some false false indications in § 10.


## About Chapter 9

76    Who, in fact, is the child in the tree?

77**  The Princess pretends that Efellel has, in fact, given an indication to the dog, who was too stupid to decipher it. Do better.

78    Put forward a hypothesis about the identity of the horrible enemy of the dog.

79    (optional) Who kidnapped Briolanja?

# Dedication of the Tale to the Princess
# by the Tail

Could one imagine, PRINCESS, putting into other hands than yours this tale, yours being the only ones worthy of receiving it?

Thou art Adventure, and the **Tale** is Algebra, eminently.

Thou art Blonde, and the **Tale** is Barbary with the sheet Blank.

Thou art ELEGANT, INSENSIBLE and the **Tale** is Irreducible Enigma.

Are you not meant to understand each other?

Besides, doesn't the tale bear both our names united in its **Title**, except for this small detail that one eye has gone from mine and been replaced, shot out in times past at the siege of Vienna by a Turkish bullet? But there is still enough left of me to save you.

In this our century, the groans of prose are nothing but sophisms. **Lyric** poetry, having always been **Mockery**, has had its days of relative legerdemain and contingent contortions. The **Tale**, only the **Tale** can speak the truth. And does speak it.

As to what else it contains and which thou refusest to acknowledge, I advise it not to Talk about it in order that from this Silence itself will burst forth in spite of thee, under the most moving *conjointness*, the terrible *sen* of my life.

At the moment of tracing these **Letters** which, completing my work, will forever declare thee to be its **Suzeraine**, a doubt comes to my mind: in so relinquishing the minute part of myself, in deciding to speak Not as Tail but, speaking on its behalf, as a Knot to the Tale, have I not committed a fatal error? Oh yes,

yes, I suddenly understand, but too late, that **SOMEONE ELSE**, without my knowledge, has slipped into the tale and, taking cowheardly advantage of the impersonality of the Adventures, is directing towards you the infamy of his desire. And you might already be listening to him, with complacency! **WHO'S SPEAKING?**

Unfortunate being that I am. What did I say? what didn't I say? what do I write? where am I? whither do I run? I am going astray

Ah PRINCESS! PRINCESS Ah Princess ah! PRINCESS!

Farewell! ah Farewell!

The Tail of Labrador

# Index

****, 101

ADAICCQTOB fourth grade Cambaceres incumbent, 22, 23, 28, 77, 126

albatross, 29, 76, 79

Alcalde, 18, 19, 65, 95

*Alice in Wonderland,* 44

ants, 19

Architect, 14

Astronomer, 20-32, 40-42, 47, 68, 75, 76-88, 108, 123

baker, 18, 95

Barbara, blue whale, 78-79, 80, 85

Bartleby, hedgehog, 18, 19, 78, 95, 96-100, 103, 117-18, 126

birds, 12, 13, 59

Bogarde, Dirk, actor, 66

Brigid, young pink California crane, 100-101

Briolanja, hedgehog, 18, 19, 95, 98-100, 118, 126

butler, 38

cat, 82-83, 84, 85, 88

child in the tree, 107-8, 126

Chrétien de Troyes, 44

Crétin, Guillaume, bell-ringer, 69

Dalida, singer, 65, 67

Danieldzoï, Arnaut, snail, 111

de Casimir, Canadian beaver, 78-79, 80, 85, 95, 96, 97, 125

Dog, the, 4-126

Efellel, Fresident-Pounder of Oulipo, 112-14, 126

emissary, 18

Epaminondas, English squirrel, 12, 59, 77-79, 85, 95, 106, 117-18

Epigone, 102

four Abyssinian white geese, 71, 95

four anteaters, 95

four baby Etruscan hippopotamuses, 71

# Separate Index

Adirondac, Queen, 11, 35, 57-58, 65, 100-101, 102

Aïda, cousin, 65-66

Aligoté, King, 8-11, 14, 16, 35, 37-40, 42, 51, 57-58, 89

Avogadr (without an o), King, 104-5

Babylas, King, 8-11, 14-20, 25, 34-35, 37-39, 42, 47, 51, 57, 90, 105

Beryl, cousin, 12-13, 15, 17-20, 31, 73

Botswanna, Queen, 11, 15, 31, 35, 38, 57-58, 90, 102-3, 104-5

damsel, a, 108-9

Desmond, King, 50-51, 58, 89-102, 124, 126

Eleonor (without an e), King, 8-11, 14, 16, 35, 37-39, 49-51, 55, 57-58, 65, 121, 123, 124

Eleonore (with an e), Queen, 11, 35, 38, 59, 60, 64, 65, 69, 102, 104

Eponyme, King, 104-5

Ermengarde, cousin, 39, 59-60, 64, 65-70, 72-74, 76, 80, 87, 125

Faraday, King, 50-53, 57, 59, 60, 65-66, 67, 68, 74, 76, 90, 94, 95, 97, 102-3, 104, 124

Gustave, King, 104-5

Hoppy, the Princess, 4-128

Imogène, King, 8-12, 14-16, 34, 36, 37-38, 49-50, 57-58, 90, 121

Ingrid, Queen, 11, 15, 31, 34, 36, 58, 90, 92, 102, 104-5

Jugurtha, King, 104-5, 117

king, a, 108-9

Marie-Josèphe, 23-28, 76, 81-88, 126

Onophriu (without an s), King, 49-51, 58, 65, 94, 95, 102, 104, 124

river, the, 13, 15, 78, 95, 96, 97, 102, 106, 117

Sol, 41, 91-92, 95

Upholep, King, 49-50, 57, 58, 90, 94, 95, 102, 104

Uther Pendragon, King, 9-10, 14, 38, 40, 69, 92, 94-95, 98

Ygerne, Queen, 14

young man, a, 108

# MORE OULIPIAN TITLES
# FROM DALKEY ARCHIVE PRESS